I0648687

Deadly Beloved

by the same author

ENTER SECOND MURDERER
BLOOD LINE

Deadly Beloved

An Inspector Faro Mystery

Alanna Knight

St. Martin's Press
New York

Library of Congress Cataloging-in-Publication Data

Knight, Alanna.
Deadly beloved / Alanna Knight.
p. cm.
"A Thomas Dunne book."
ISBN 0-312-05069-0
I. Title.
PR6061.N45D4 1990
823'.914—dc20 90-36885
CIP

First published in Great Britain by Macmillan London Limited

First U.S. Edition: October 1990

10 9 8 7 6 5 4 3 2 1

In memory of Elizabeth Byrd

Chapter One

Two weeks after the police surgeon's wife vanished on a train journey from Edinburgh to North Berwick, when all enquiries discreet but exhaustive had failed, the first grim evidence appeared. A bloodstained fur cloak and kitchen carving knife, discovered in the melting snow near the railway line at Longniddry Station, were ominous indications that the case could no longer be regarded as a 'missing persons' enquiry.

Who could have imagined a furore over the burnt roast at a dinner party as prelude to another sordid domestic crime?

Such were Detective Inspector Jeremy Faro's thoughts as he painstakingly sifted through memory's tedious details of the evening's events.

Aware from long experience that the first place one searched for a motive to murder was within the victim's family circle, he concluded that it had been a very dull party indeed. Until Mrs Eveline Shaw went to the piano and played the Beethoven Appassionata. Up to that moment boredom, rather than the very modest amount of indifferent wine served at the police surgeon's table, was responsible for the blunting of Faro's normally keen powers of observation.

Once upon a time he had believed that mayhem and murder, his daily round and common task with the Edinburgh City Police, were confined to the criminal world. Now he knew that the miasma of molten corruption, seething from grim wynds and tall 'lands' under the

Castle's ancient shadow, could no longer be confined to those wretches who stole and stabbed and procured and perverted.

In recent times crime stalked the respectable New Town, like some ghastly retribution by the ghosts of all those he had hunted down and brought to justice. Now it seemed that their evil shades threatened to roost in the circle of his own family and friends. He would have hesitated to include Dr Melville Kellar in the category of personal friend, but here was a crime brushing uneasily close to 9 Sheridan Place and his own hearth. His stepson Dr Vincent Beaumarcher Laurie was the police surgeon's assistant and the confidant of the missing woman.

Without having the least pretentions to medical diagnosis, Faro had recognised for several weeks before the event that his stepson was suffering from a malady of the heart. Secretive, vague and preoccupied, Vince was displaying all the symptoms of romantic involvement. Faro wondered if the sudden decision to take a short holiday with his doctor friend Walter in the Austrian asylum for consumptives was a sensible retreat, a prudent flight into neutral territory that would give him time to get his emotions into the right perspective.

It was not, however, until after Vince's return from Vienna and Faro's disclosures concerning the missing woman, that he learned with surprise and misgiving that the object of his stepson's affection was Mabel Kellar.

Vince's face had paled as he listened. 'I can't believe this, Stepfather. You must be mistaken. Couldn't she have had an accident? Lost her memory?'

'That was our first thought, lad.'

'You've tried the hospitals?'

'Aye, and the workhouses too.'

'I visited her the morning after the dinner party, to say goodbye before I went on holiday,' Vince whispered in awed tones. 'She was preparing to leave, to visit her sister in North Berwick. It's dreadful, dreadful. Unbelievable.'

Faro poured a large whisky and handed it to his stepson. 'Drink this and when you're feeling calmer, we'll talk about it.'

'Calmer? Oh dear God! Who would want to harm her? She was one of the sweetest, kindest creatures on this earth. I loved her, yes, loved her, Stepfather,' he added defiantly. 'I would have died for her.'

Faro said nothing, inclined to dismiss his stepson's infatuation for what it was: the inevitable attraction to a mother figure. Mabel Kellar was older than his own mother, Lizzie Faro, would have been and Vince, determined to avoid matrimony at all costs, had chosen yet another love where no lasting commitment was possible.

'She had no enemies. Everyone who knew her loved her,' said Vince.

The evidence, thought Faro grimly, suggested that someone had hated her. Hated her enough to destroy her.

Later Vince gave Faro an account of that last visit.

'Thinking about it now, I realise that she was considerably agitated. Very upset. There had been yet another unholy row with Kellar after the guests departed. Serious enough for her to be seeking refuge with her sister. Actually leaving her husband, as he rightly deserves. She should have done so long ago, if she hadn't slavishly adored him.'

'What was this row about? Did she tell you?'

'She spared me the exact details, hinted at a very unpleasant post-mortem on the culinary disasters of the dinner. Kellar blamed her entirely for her unfortunate choice of housekeeper. I offered to escort her to the railway station as I was catching a train there myself, but she refused. She wasn't quite ready to leave. Packing to complete, instructions to leave and so forth. Oh dear God – I can't . . . ' And Vince, covering his face, began to sob.

Faro put a compassionate hand on his shoulder. 'There, there, lad.' He felt the words were inadequate to deal with his stepson's unrequited passion, since Mabel Kellar had adored only her husband.

Melville Kellar occupied a position of authority with the Edinburgh City Police. He was highly respected and esteemed, although Vince's daily grumblings painted a picture of a harsh disciplinarian, bigoted and intolerant of human error and inefficiency. Pompous and overbearing, Dr Kellar emerged as utterly callous in his dealings with medical students. Perhaps in order to sleep well at nights, the police surgeon had of necessity retreated into a remote unfeeling shell, a refuge denied Faro, aware that even if he was spared to serve with the City Police for another twenty years, he would never become accustomed to scenes of bloody murder, or be unmoved at a life hideously snuffed out by sudden violent death.

'Kellar could give his dissecting knives lessons in sharpness,' the students who endured his sarcasm were wont to say. And not only students, thought Faro. The honest peeler walking the beat and the hard-working underpaid domestic within the Kellar kitchen existed on a separate plane. They belonged to a sub-species he never cared to let his eyes dwell upon or acknowledge as fellow human beings with the same capacity for joy and suffering as himself. There was a rumour that, in common with Royalty, Dr Kellar expected domestics to stay out of sight unless summoned to appear.

'If he comes face-to-face with a servant going about her duties, he'll dismiss her on the spot. What do you think of that, Stepfather?'

'If it's true, it's incredible.'

Prior to the dinner party, Faro's encounters with Kellar had been limited to the police mortuary, where his first impression had been of a man slightly below middle height with piercing blue eyes, who made up for his lack of stature with a biting tongue and a high opinion of his own lofty intellectual stature.

In Kellar's eyes, even senior detectives were mindless fools.

Faro still recalled uncomfortably the occasion when

he had ventured an opinion about the cause of a victim's death at a post-mortem.

Kellar had rounded upon him, eyes flashing, brows lowered like a charging bull.

'Are you questioning my findings, sir? Are you insinuating from your somewhat meagre education in forensic matters that you are more capable of an effective diagnosis in this case . . . '

Faro had wilted beneath that volley of invective. As it turned out, his theory was proved correct and Kellar was quick to bask in all the praise without the slightest qualm of conscience. Apology never occurred to him or acknowledgement of the Detective Inspector's shrewd observations which had led to the capture and subsequent sentencing of the murderer.

Faro shrugged such incidents aside, realising how they could influence his own judgement. In his profession, prejudice could be fatal to the fair-mindedness that was the very essence of justice.

To be entirely fair, the gruesome daily round at the mortuary presented the surgeon in a very different guise to the host in full evening dress, presiding over the dinner table.

Faro was at once struck by Kellar's commanding appearance which might well have awed his medical students, who would not necessarily have noticed that their tormentor was good-looking in a silver-haired distinguished way, allying the chilly classical features of a marble Greek god with a smile that was charm itself.

His smiles that evening, however, were as rare as his replenishment of the guests' wine glasses, too long empty for politeness and indicating that rumour was true. Kellar was tight-fisted and his wife down-trodden and pathetic.

'A somewhat ill-assorted pair, didn't you think?' he asked Vince.

'I know what you're thinking,' was the defensive reply.

'Mabel was an heiress and he had married her for her money.'

Faro shrugged. Handsome men often married plain wives. And Mabel Kellar's exterior did indeed hide a heart of gold, if appearances were anything to go by. He had been touched by her devotion to her protegée, Mrs Shaw, that young and beautiful woman scarce past girlhood.

After lighting a pipe, Faro poured himself a dram and when Mrs Brook had cleared the supper table, he found his concentration wandering from the police report on a fraud case he had recently successfully brought to justice.

One thought persisted, refusing to be ignored. He had the gift, not always a happy one, of being able to put himself squarely in other men's shoes. In Dr Kellar's case, had his wife gone missing then surely the first places he would have searched, after hammering anxiously on the doors of close friends and relations, were the hospitals.

There was always the possibility in view of the damning evidence that she had been attacked on the train and flung out of the carriage. There were also several other alarming possibilities which suggested that if she was still alive she might be very seriously injured. As police surgeon, Kellar enjoyed a unique advantage in having easy access to discreet perusal of hospital admissions and a look into their wards if necessary.

And yet he had failed to do so. Why? And Faro's thoughts returned again to the events of the Kellars' last dinner party. In a pattern that was familiar after twenty years of fighting crime, he found himself meticulously examining every detail of that evening, searching for the first clue into the labyrinth, imagining his host in the role of potential wife-murderer.

Only two weeks ago . . .

Chapter Two

Dr Kellar and his wife lived in a handsome mansion in the Grange, in the recently developed south side of Edinburgh. Built at the beginning of Victoria's reign, strenuous efforts had been made to make it look considerably older. Nothing had been spared in mediaeval turrets, Gothic flourishes of gargoyles and even hints at a drawbridge and studded door.

As an architectural purist, a stickler for the clean lines and uncomplicated plans of the Georgian era, Faro dismissed the result as yet another nightmare in domestic architecture.

'Have you ever noticed,' he asked Vince, as the hired carriage bounded down the drive, its myriad twists and turns designed to establish in the minds of arriving guests an illusion of parkland and a rich man's estate. 'Have you ever noticed,' he repeated, 'how often houses resemble their owners?'

Vince laughed. 'Never. Aren't you confusing your similes? I thought that particular one referred to dogs and pets only. Come, Stepfather, not so glum. You'll enjoy meeting Mabel Kellar. And I'm sure there'll be excellent food and wine, and grand company too.'

The first snowflakes were falling as they pressed the bell a second time. Faro, dragging up his greatcoat collar, tapped his foot impatiently. 'What on earth can be keeping them? One would imagine an army of servants lurking about such an establishment.'

He was to discover that servants were almost non-existent at the best of times, Dr Kellar's excuse being that he couldn't abide such creatures and more than an absolute minimum posed a dire threat to his privacy.

At last the door was opened by the housekeeper, her flour-covered hands explaining the delay. A lady of ample proportions in starched apron and large white cap over untidy wisps of grey hair, her chin was swathed in a large muffler.

'Come in. Missus will be with you in a wee minute,' she whispered hoarsely and indicated the staircase. 'You'll find master up there, drawing-room, first door left.'

At that moment, Dr Kellar appeared on the landing. 'Is that Flynn down there?'

The housekeeper with a nervous hand adjusted her spectacles and bobbed a curtsey. 'Yes, sir.'

'Your place is below stairs, Flynn. Where is your mistress?'

'In the kitchen, sir.'

'I want her here – at once. Does she not know the guests have arrived?' And for the two visitors staring up at him with some embarrassment, he summoned a wintry smile. 'Come away, gentlemen. Come away.'

After they climbed the stairs, he greeted them with an apology. 'My wife employs local domestics and allows them home at the weekend.'

This indulgence was not, as it appeared, out of kindness, Vince told Faro later, but because Kellar's chronic meanness made him suspect servants of stealing food and so forth. Most men in his position would keep a resident coachman, too, but the luxury of board and meagre lodgings was the sole perquisite of the housekeeper.

As for the excellent company, Vince had been sadly mistaken and Faro was dismayed to discover their fellow guests were Superintendent McIntosh of the Edinburgh City Police and his waspish wife, known irreverently in the Central Office as The Tartar.

Faro suppressed a sigh. He had few off-duty hours,

especially as criminals took full advantage of the possibilities offered by long dark winter nights. He had no desire to spend one of his precious free evenings in the company of his superior, a man he found opinionated and tiresome at the best of times. McIntosh's acknowledgement, briefer than courtesy prescribed, spoke volumes on his own astonishment and displeasure at seeing Inspector Faro.

As Kellar ushered them into the drawing-room, Faro observed, sitting at the grand piano, an extremely pretty young woman in deep mourning. Since Kellar did not deign to introduce her, Faro presumed that this was a poor relative, recently widowed, and doubtless regarded by the doctor as just one more mouth to feed.

The atmosphere was less than cordial and Faro was heartily glad when the distant doorbell announced another arrival. A few moments later Mrs Kellar ushered in Sir Hedley Marsh.

Known in the Newington district as the Mad Bart, he was the last person Faro and Vince expected to encounter at the lofty police surgeon's dining-table. Their exchange of puzzled glances was a wordless comment on this odd company of dinner guests. How had the hermit of Solomon's Tower been lured away from his army of cats?

Faro looked sharply at his hostess. Since it was well known that Sir Hedley despised and avoided all human contact, perhaps Mrs Kellar did have extraordinary powers of attraction, not evident at first glance. Despite Vince's commendations, he was to remember no lasting impression when it was vital to do so. He recalled a plain woman, tall and thin with dark hair pulled tightly back from indeterminate features. What colour were her eyes, was her nose short or long, her face round or oval?

Faro shook his head. Even details of the elaborate velvet gown had vanished. Was it blue or green? The colour was unimportant for it served only to emphasise her lack of style, while her fingernails testified to her agitation, bearing traces of her recent domestic activity in the kitchen.

Another surprise was still to come, for the Mad Bart had been introduced as: 'My dear Uncle Hedley.'

As they shook hands Faro decided that although Sir Hedley's dress was correct for the occasion, albeit a little out of date, he had not escaped completely from his cats after all. He had, at close quarters, brought their ripe odours with him.

'I believe you two know each other already,' said Mrs Kellar.

'We do. Inspector and I are near neighbours. How d'ye-do?'

Mrs Kellar smiled. 'And I might add, Inspector, you are the chief reason for Uncle Hedley accepting our invitation.'

Sir Hedley grinned sheepishly. 'Like good conversation. See you often passing by. Haven't chatted since you took one of my kits. Big fella now?'

'Yes, indeed.'

Sir Hedley nodded vigorously. 'Gave him a name, I hope.'

'Rusty.'

'Rusty, eh. Like it. Like it. Good mouser?'

'Very.' And aware of the old man's frowning glances in Vince's direction: 'Let me introduce you to my stepson, Dr Vincent Laurie.'

Faro suppressed a smile. He detected a certain distaste as the fastidious young doctor took the extended and none-too-clean hand.

'From these parts, are you, young fella?'

'I've lived in Edinburgh for most of my life, sir.'

Sir Hedley frowned. 'We've met before, of course. What kind of a doctor are you?'

Vince was saved a reply as Mabel Kellar ushered the young widow towards them. 'Now, Uncle, you can talk as much as you like at dinner. I want dear Vince to talk to my dearest friend and companion, Mrs Eveline Shaw.'

Not a poor relative after all, thought Faro, observing

Mrs Kellar watching benignly as Vince and Mrs Shaw shook hands.

'The Superintendent is waiting to meet you, Uncle Hedley,' said Kellar and led the old man, glowering ferociously, in the direction of the waiting McIntoshes. Turning, he addressed Mrs Kellar: 'I take it that dinner is ready? Will you lead the way?'

Formal etiquette demanded that Dr Kellar lead in Mrs McIntosh; the Superintendent took in Mrs Shaw and as Sir Hedley was intent on questioning Vince rather loudly, Faro brought up the rear, offering Mrs Kellar his arm.

'You will be nice to Uncle Hedley, won't you?' she whispered.

'I will, indeed. You are to be congratulated on getting him out of Solomon's Tower. Quite extraordinary.'

Mrs Kellar laughed. 'Don't I know it! But as I said, I have you to thank – and the Superintendent.'

'Indeed?'

'Yes, he is absolutely fascinated by crime. He's a great admirer of yours. And so am I, Inspector. I have heard so much about you from dear Vince. You have such kind eyes. You don't look at all like a policeman.'

Faro intercepted the long glance over a fluttering fan, a look that in any other woman he would have considered highly coquettish. Embarrassed, he chuckled: 'Indeed? I don't know quite how to answer that one, ma'am. What, pray, do policeman look like? "If you prick us, do we not bleed? if you tickle us, do we not laugh? if you poison us, do we not die? and if you wrong us, shall we not revenge?"'

Mrs Kellar did not acknowledge his smiling glance. She was staring straight ahead, white-faced, her expression one of sudden terror.

'Ma'am?' said Faro gently.

The fan had closed and was clutched tightly between white-knuckled fists.

'Ma'am?' he repeated gently, ushering her towards the table.

Suddenly aware of him, the fan fluttered free again and she laughed. 'Dear Vince told me of your passion for Shakespeare. Did you see Sir Henry Irving in *The Merchant*?'

'I did indeed.'

'Are we not very privileged to have his annual visit to Edinburgh? We never miss a performance.'

Acutely aware as he was of changes in atmosphere, Faro had sensed a dangerous moment, and wondered upon whom that dark glance had fallen. Now as he seated her at the table, she tapped him on the wrist.

'Not ma'am, Inspector. You must please call me Mabel – as your dear Vince does. For I hope we are also to be friends.'

On the other side of the table Vince suppressed a smile, conscious of the admiring glances of both Mabel Kellar and Eveline Shaw in his stepfather's direction.

Faro, so shrewd and observant, could never see himself as he appeared to others, thought Vince, especially to the ladies – certainly not as a sober widower approaching forty and therefore to be dismissed as thoroughly ineligible. True, his interest in dress was negligible, but despite his declaration that the only function of clothes was a decent covering for nakedness, he managed by instinct to choose the right thing to wear.

Examining his stepfather feature by feature, Vince noted the heavy silver-gilt hair and the wide-set dark blue eyes of the psychic. They didn't look *at* you, but right *into* you as if they read a fellow's very soul, a fact which many a criminal had found disconcerting. True, his nose was rather long and his lips were thinner than made for beauty but that was out of the habit of pressing them together in contemplation rather than their natural shape.

He had inherited good looks and a splendid physique from his Orkney ancestors, but there the resemblance to those fierce warriors ended. Vince, from the threshold of youth, had long guessed the secret of the Inspector's attraction to the opposite sex: an irresistible combination of those qualities which appealed to women, strength and reliability with that most disarming of manly features, a gentle smile and a compassionate heart. Here was a strong man who could also cry and was not ashamed of his tears.

Vince's attention was distracted from his stepfather as Dr Kellar poured the wine and Mrs Kellar excused herself.

'Mabel,' bellowed her husband from the other end of the table. 'Mabel, where are you going now?'

'Just to the kitchen, my love. To look at the oven.'

'Can't Flynn take care of that?'

'I've told you, dearest, she's most unwell.' And to the guests she fluttered nervous hands. 'The poor creature. She has such a cruel toothache. You saw her, didn't you? Her face all swollen?'

The guests murmured sympathetically and Mrs Kellar continued: 'I couldn't possibly ask her to prepare dinner, swooning with agony.'

'Go on then, woman, but hurry up,' was Kellar's ungracious dismissal. And as the door closed, 'I must apologise. My wife is too indulgent. She thrives on waifs and strays.'

Sir Hedley squeezed Faro's arm and whispered hoarsely, 'He means me. Doesn't like me much. Came for Mabel's sake.'

But Faro observed that the barb had also been intended for another guest, as he caught Dr Kellar's hooded glance in the direction of Mrs Shaw, who studied her plate intently.

The food served failed to come up to Vince's hints of excellence; it was uninspired, insipid and disappointing to both men used as they were to their housekeeper Mrs Brook's abundant and excellent cooking.

Faro could, however, sympathise more than most with Mrs Flynn's problem. He knew all about the agonies of toothache since he frequently cornered desperate and violent criminals and disarmed them of deadly weapons with considerably more aplomb than he ever faced a dental surgeon's chair.

Considering the housekeeper's malady which necessitated their hostess's frequent excursion below stairs to give 'a hand', Faro, a kind and sympathetic employer himself, would have readily overlooked tepid soup and the long delays between courses, had the wine – even Dr Kellar's somewhat substandard table wine – continued to flow in agreeable abundance.

After a longer wait than usual, during which the guests, and Sir Hedley in particular, with much clearing of the throat stared meaningfully into empty glasses, Mrs Kellar reappeared looking warm and flustered, bearing before her a serving dish from which blue smoke issued forth.

Dr Kellar sniffed the air and, it seemed in retrospect to Faro, looked up quite murderously from the task of sharpening his carving knives, an action which he had carried out with the pride and expertise to be expected of a brilliant surgeon. Later Faro was to wish he had paid a little more attention to those knives, one of which went a-missing and whose reappearance in sinister and dramatic circumstances was to play a vital part in the murder evidence.

Overcome with rage, Dr Kellar had shouted, 'This is an outrage – and I hold you directly responsible, Mabel. We seldom have guests to dinner these days and when we do, I expect perfection. Perfection, do you hear, madam? Intolerable food and intolerable serving, a housekeeper who cannot even cook a decent meal! This is an unforgivable insult to our guests—'

'Her references were quite excellent, my dear, you read them yourself and approved,' Mrs Kellar interrupted defensively. 'Please be patient, she has such dreadful toothache, in awful agonies.'

'Then she must see a dental surgeon and have it extracted.'

A delicate shudder passed round the table. Faro was not alone in his cowardice.

'Yes, have it ripped out,' Kellar continued, 'But not on my time,' he roared, thumping the table. 'I have had quite enough of her. Enough. I do not pay domestics to indulge themselves with petty indispositions. You are to give her a week's notice immediately. Do you hear, woman, one week's notice.'

'But what are we to do?' wailed Mrs Kellar. 'We cannot be left without help in the house.'

'Then set about finding a replacement.'

'Please be reasonable, my love. I cannot possibly find anyone in a week.'

'One week,' thundered Kellar. 'You have one week. And that is my last word on the subject, madam.'

'As you wish, my love.'

In the heavy silence that followed, Mrs Kellar's sniffs indicated barely suppressed tears while the guests did their best to avoid each other's eyes. They concentrated in a half-hearted way on staring ahead at nothing in particular, resisting at all costs a curious or speculative glance in the direction of the ruined roast, still smouldering like a burnt offering on the centre of the table.

'And where is our maid this evening?' demanded Dr Kellar.

'You allowed Ina home for the weekend. Don't you remember, my dear – that is our usual procedure.' Mrs Kellar looked round the table, her helpless gesture begging affirmation and approval.

'Hrmmph,' growled Dr Kellar, his indignant shake of the head indicating that this generous impulse had been ungratefully reciprocated.

Emboldened, Mrs Kellar went on: 'And might I remind you, my dear, that the necessity for acquiring a new housekeeper need never have arisen, had you not given Mrs Freeman notice.' Again she appealed to the guests: 'Mrs Freeman's services gave no cause for complaint, an admirable housekeeper in every way.'

'A self-opinionated fool,' sneered Kellar. 'And rude. Damnably rude.'

'You forget, my love, that she had looked after this

house for nearly thirty years and regarded it as her own.'

'Hrmmph. Small disagreement, that was all. Ungrateful wretch left in a huff without working her notice. No character need she expect from me, nor this new one either. You may tell her that, as a parting gift.' Kellar's sneer as he continued to flourish the carving knife now assumed sinister and monstrous significance.

Faro shrugged aside such imaginings. A ruined meal, problems with the servants, were hardly just cause and impediment for murdering one's spouse. If that were the case, then the daily press would have no news of anything else but domestic crimes.

The dessert, an apple tart also somewhat charred about the edges, was served plus a Scotch trifle sadly lacking in sherry as its main flavouring.

There was a momentary revival of cheerful spirits around the table as the guests noted the appearance of the port decanter.

Faro declined the cheese and concentrated on trying to attract Vince's attention, wondering how soon they could decently and discreetly excuse themselves. His hopes sank when Mabel announced: 'Our dear friend Mrs Shaw has been prevailed upon to play for us very shortly. She is an excellent performer,' she added reassuringly.

As there was no possibility of bringing the evening to a close, Faro considered his host dispassionately. Dr Kellar was a snob and worse, a pompous parsimonious bore whose choice of conversation seemed limited to promoting his own importance to the Edinburgh City Police with the addition of graphic descriptions relating to his dissections of interesting cadavers of criminals past and present. The mere flicker of an eyelid from Vince indicated to Faro that they were in agreement about the suitability of this topic for light dinner-table conversation.

Despite Vince's high commendation of their hostess, none of her sterling qualities was evident and Mabel Kellar was soon to retreat into a blurred memory, a well-meaning bungling nonentity, her sole virtues being to suffer incompetent servants gladly and acquiring waifs and strays.

When she wasn't scuttling back and forth to the kitchen, Faro observed that her attentions were devoted almost exclusively to Vince and Eveline Shaw. Her colour grew more hectic as she beamed upon them, pressing the young woman's hand affectionately or patting her cheek with her fan.

The specially-invited Uncle Hedley, sitting next to Vince, was being studiously ignored by that young man, intent upon discussing with his hostess his imminent trip to Vienna.

On Sir Hedley's other side, Superintendent McIntosh was enthusiastically following his host's dismemberment of cadavers while the Mad Bart looked bewildered and very glum indeed. Faro, after a few vain attempts to engage him in conversation across the wide table, gave up and regarded the scene thoughtfully.

Again he was struck by the ill-chosen assortment of dinner guests, puzzled by the reason for his inclusion. This first social invitation to the police surgeon's house was flattering but obscure, since they had little to say to one another, and before tonight he would have considered that their dislike was mutual.

He turned his attention to Vince and Eveline Shaw, clucked over in a nervous mother-hen fashion by Mabel Kellar. The thought sprang to his mind unbidden: had this dinner party been carefully planned as an occasion for matchmaking between the dearest friend and companion and his young stepson who was Mabel's confidant? Was that why the pleasure of his company had been required, to give approval and blessing? The thought was firmly rooted in reality, for matchmaking was the main creative hobby of Edinburgh matrons in Mabel Kellar's stratum of society. Faro imagined that just such a scene might be encountered at other Edinburgh dinner tables this evening, presided over by many an anxious mama, desperate to find a husband for a daughter no longer young, and whose face had never been her fortune.

As for Eveline Shaw herself, oblivious and indifferent to being the centre of her hostess's adulations, her attitude was one of sadness and patient bewilderment. She stared at her plate and spoke little apart from accepting or declining the food offered, her mourning dress serving only to enhance that young and lovely face.

Faro shook his head. No. Mrs Shaw wouldn't do at all for Vince. Small wonder he preferred his hostess. But what could have united these two women, so dissimilar, in friendship? The young widow, stricken and lost in the lachrymose stage of early bereavement, appeared to be scarcely older than Vince. Faro guessed that she had not been married long and was no doubt still deeply in love with her dead husband.

He knew all about losing one's beloved partner and sympathised silently with the countenance frozen in unhappiness across the table. Her expression suggested that she longed for the solitude of her own home, to be alone with her melancholy thoughts. Her silence and lack of spontaneity told a tale of bitter regret at having been persuaded to accept Mabel Kellar's thinly veiled invitation, and all its implications, to be jolly and meet 'the nice young doctor.'

Was her 'dearest friend and companion's' refusal to cooperate in the matchmaking activity, the plan that had gone awry, the reason for Mrs Kellar's distraught appearance? There was more in it than that. Faro had observed the fleeting glance of terror displayed earlier by Mrs Kellar. Mrs Shaw was also afraid.

Faro was to remember the significance of that moment when he endeavoured to deduce the sinister elements and motives lurking behind the masks worn by the guests at that very dull and chaotic dinner party.

His attention was drawn repeatedly to Sir Hedley. He

was not frightened but certainly appeared ill-at-ease. His attempts to engage Vince or the Superintendent in conversation had been rather discourteously ignored. What was his reason for being included? Surely more than an obligation to his niece and a fascination with crime had been required to persuade him out of that hermit's shell in Solomon's Tower?

Had he been invited out of thoughtful concern or simply to make up the sitting? Whatever the reason, the old man must have been concluding that it was all a dismal failure, thought Faro, turning his attention to Superintendent McIntosh.

A toady of the worst possible kind, McIntosh hung on every word Kellar uttered.

'A little bird tells me that there is a knighthood in the offing, Doctor. Let me be the first to offer my congratulations.'

Faro shuddered. Coyness sat ill upon the Superintendent's fleshy shoulders and Kellar's attempt at modest indifference also failed. He beamed.

'That is so. Word has newly reached me. But in the utmost confidence.' He put a finger to his lips. 'Not a word. I know I can rely on your discretion, Superintendent. Not one word.'

'You may rely on me utterly, Doctor. Utterly.'

Faro suppressed a smile. The forthcoming knighthood was common knowledge and he suspected that every policeman walking the High Street in Edinburgh was betting on its probability.

'How absolutely thrilling, Doctor Kellar,' put in Mrs McIntosh. 'And such an honour for your dear wife too.'

The dear wife alerted, looked momentarily more distraught as Mrs McIntosh endeavoured to gain her attention.

Faro had early decided that for Mrs McIntosh the evening would be memorable as a social triumph. True, she did not inhabit the same intellectual plane as her host but she shared his abominable snobbery, and was rosy with delight at finding herself dining with a Title and a Knight-To-Be. Her gushing attempts to converse with Sir Hedley had not met with much success, as the latter apparently failed to hear, or was deaf to the shrill remarks directed toward him.

Mrs McIntosh was two inches under five feet tall but she made up for her small stature by a massive temper, and her angry glances boded ill for her spouse who had twice interrupted her flow of eloquence on the one subject dear to her heart.

She understood, oh, how she understood and sympathised with dear Dr Kellar's outburst of passion on the subject of new housekeepers. She knew, oh, how she knew all about domestics and how hard they were to come by. And oh dear me, such low creatures they were these days, one would imagine they would be grateful for the chance to shelter under the same roof as their betters.

'You cannot get a good girl, a really good girl, cheap to live in anywhere these days. They actually demand wages in return for bed and board. Do you not find it so, Sir Hedley?'

The Mad Bart's eyes swivelled nervously in the direction of Vince and Mabel Kellar. With an exasperated sigh Mrs McIntosh turned to Faro. 'Now you must agree with me, Inspector. Servants must be of crucial importance for the smooth running of an Inspector's household.'

'I give the matter little attention, madam,' said Faro coldly.

'Of course, I understand you are fortunate in having that nice little Mrs Brook. We tried to get her to come to us – did you know that? – when her dear doctor, her former employer at Sheridan Place, died so suddenly . . . '

But Faro was no longer listening, thinking venomously of how he could remove that simpering glance with the information that his own dear Lizzie had been a domestic servant who had an illegitimate son – Vince – as a result of being raped by one of the so-called gentry when she was fifteen years old.

Vince. He looked at his stepson fondly wondering, as he often did, if the boy had been his own child, whether he could have loved him better or found a more faithful and devoted son. Watching him animated and attentive to Mabel Kellar after rather rudely fending off Sir Hedley's attempts to be included in the conversation, Faro's qualms about the boy's happiness came again to the fore.

There was something too vulnerable about that bright head of curls, the gentle smile, a sensitive quality at odds with the grim medical task of assistant to the police surgeon. Somehow he could never imagine Vince ever acquiring the hard shell of Dr Kellar.

The clock seemed to have stopped on the mantelpiece as the meal dragged on to its weary conclusion and Mrs Kellar announced that the entertainment would now begin.

Entertainment, thought Faro. What a word to describe Mabel Kellar's monologue, 'A Sunday Afternoon Picnic', in which a whole family, celebrating Grandmama's birthday, took to the river and encountered many a storm, of the teacup variety. Mabel Kellar's change of voice for her bewilderingly large cast of characters left him stunned, his eyelids heavy. Later, he learned from Vince that this was her party piece. It seemed endless.

At last, she curtseyed delightedly to applause polite but feeble.

'Our dear Mrs Shaw will now play for us.'

Faro suppressed a bout of yawning and, with an irresistible desire to close his eyes, tried to focus his dwindling attention on the young woman as she sat down at the piano.

A few chords and he was wide awake, alert, his senses singing as he recognised Beethoven's Appassionata brilliantly executed. One of his favourite pieces, he knew that this was no bungling amateur but a pianist whose rightful place was on the concert platform.

'Bravo, bravo,' he called as the final notes faded into silence. 'Encore, encore.'

The guests who did not share his knowledge of music or his enthusiasm looked mildly dazed by his reaction. Mrs Shaw regarded him gratefully, bowed modestly and then firmly closed the piano.

He went over to her side. 'That was superb, Mrs Shaw. Beethoven at his very best.'

'You are familiar with the piece, Inspector?'

'I am indeed. And you played it divinely.'

'Why, thank you. Thank you.' Animation transformed her face into sudden radiance and Faro saw fleetingly how captivating she must have been in the days before sadness engulfed her, swamping her young life.

And just when the evening had begun for him, Faro heard the doorbell. The carriages had arrived. As cloaks were gathered, Dr Kellar opened the front door to a moon gleaming fitfully and a gentle snowfall.

Mrs Kellar took an affectionate farewell of her dearest friend whom Vince handed into the carriage bound for Regent Crescent. Faro bowed gallantly over her hand. 'Thank you again for your exquisite playing, Mrs Shaw.'

A sweet smile, a kiss blown in her hostess's direction and she was gone. Faro observed that Mrs Kellar had taken Vince's arm and now kissed him, very tenderly, on both cheeks.

Sir Hedley, bound for Solomon's Tower, was disposed to linger. Watching Vince with that hooded intense look he said earnestly, 'Enjoyed meeting you, young fella. Drop into the Tower. Any time. Always welcome.'

'Thank you, sir. But I'm fearfully busy. You must excuse me.'

Faro noticed that Vince could barely conceal his distaste. He withdrew his hand from Sir Hedley's in a gesture almost too hasty for politeness. Again struck by this unreasonable aversion to a sad lonely old man, so unlike his charitable stepson who was fond of everyone and was charming and popular, Faro frowned uneasily. He felt as if he was witnessing a resurrection of the spoilt ill-mannered small boy he had first encountered during his courtship of Vince's mother.

The absence of a carriage for Faro and Vince was another catastrophe for Mrs Kellar.

'We will enjoy the walk home.'

'But look at the snow. My dear, you must not catch a chill,' said Mrs Kellar, stroking Vince's arm anxiously. 'Do please accept Uncle Hedley's offer.'

'The exercise is good for us both, isn't it, lad?'

'It is indeed. Doctor's orders, Stepfather,' said Vince, with a look of gratitude. As they raised their hats to the departing carriages and set off down the drive, he said, 'I hope you don't mind, truly, Stepfather.'

'Not in the least.'

'The idea of sharing a carriage with that dreadful old man gives me the shivers. I absolutely loathe him.'

'That's a bit strong, lad.'

'So was the smell of cats. Don't tell me you didn't notice. I thought I'd succeeded in putting him in his place, when he kept trying so rudely to corner me with his wretched conversation. I was appalled at having to sit beside him. But tell me, what did you think of Eveline Shaw? Isn't she a stunner?'

Faro gave him a sharp look. Had he completely misread the signs? Was Vince about to confess devotion to the young widow?

'She's certainly lovely and such a talented musician.'

'Absolutely first class. I wonder where she learned to play like that?'

'How long has she been a widow?'

'Less than a year.'

'I thought so. She seemed so sad and detached.'

'Until she began to play, Stepfather. Then she was transformed.'

'You thought so too. What happened to the husband? Had she been married long?'

'Long enough to have a baby. There's a son and heir at least, a few months old, born after his soldier father was killed on the Indian frontier.'

Faro nodded sympathetically. 'Tragic. At least he left her comfortably off if she can afford a house in Regent Crescent.'

'Indeed. He was a Captain, and I gather there are very good family connections in the Highlands.'

'I'm glad to know that she'll be well provided for,' Faro hesitated and then added, 'although I doubt she will be a widow long. A wealthy widow, young and pretty too, should experience no difficulty in finding another husband.'

'Not in the least, if she is seeking one. And that I seriously doubt at the moment.' Vince laughed. 'I know you are looking very arch, Stepfather. Bless me, you are almost as bad as Mabel and I can read exactly the way your minds drift. Anyway, there were no signals in my direction, I can assure you. Not that I wanted any,' he added hastily. 'I don't see myself as a widow's consolation and I'm much too vain to play second fiddle to the dear departed.'

They walked for a while in silence then Vince said, 'There is something odd about her, didn't you think?'

'Mrs Shaw? Just lost and bewildered, lad, that's all. Isn't quite up to taking on the social round again, poor lass. Not interested in anything yet outside her own grief.'

'How perceptive of you, Stepfather. I'm relieved to hear that was the reason. You know I got a distinct impression that she didn't take to me at all, or any of us – except you.'

'Only because I appreciated her playing.'

'Oh, you do underestimate yourself, Stepfather. I despair of you sometimes, really I do.'

'Was that the first time you'd met?' asked Faro with a brisk change of subject.

'Yes. But I feel as if we're already well acquainted. Mabel talks constantly about her dear Eveline, calls her "my sister of the spirit". With no children of her own, she says the good Lord has compensated by giving her this one loving young friend.'

'Perhaps she should make it two now.'

'Two? How so?'

Faro smiled. 'Obviously Mrs Kellar regards you in the same fond light.'

'Dear Mabel. But everyone is important to her, servants, poor relatives. Fancy giving that dreadful mad old man house room. Fancy him actually being her uncle. Incredible.'

'Kellar has certainly kept very quiet about that particular skeleton in the family closet.'

'I don't suppose he's keen to have it made public, even if it is just a connection by marriage. However, it would have to come out some day. He was at great pains to tell everyone that Mabel is his heiress. There's no knowing what she'll inherit besides a multitude of cats,' Vince added. 'Solomon's Tower is fairly ruinous.'

'Yes, but don't forget, it's also on a valuable site for this upsurge of property developing in Newington area.'

As they reached the gates of Sheridan Place, Faro found himself haunted by a picture of Mabel Kellar standing on the front steps, blowing a kiss to Vince.

'Goodnight, Inspector. Goodnight, dear Vince, have a good holiday.'

A final wave as Dr Kellar drew her inside and closed the door.

And that, thought Faro, coming back to the present and his unwritten report, was the last time any of us saw the police surgeon's wife.

'Kellar is an absolute swine, treating her like that, in front of guests.' And with a chill feeling of disaster, he remembered Vince's concluding words: 'I could have snatched up one of those knives and plunged it into his black heart.'

But perhaps it was the warm-hearted Mabel who had been the victim of an assassin's carving knife.

Chapter Three

The house had seemed strangely empty without young Vince's presence. In the longest separation since they had come to live in Sheridan Place, Faro realised that this was a prelude to the future when, sooner or later, he must face the prospect of living alone.

Reasonably, he could hardly expect to have Vince with him for the rest of his life. Whatever his stepson's protestations, Faro had little doubt and fervently hoped that he would eventually fall in love and marry some suitable young lady. His wife, however, might be expected to produce excellent and convincing arguments against sharing their home with her husband's policeman stepfather.

Faro said as much to Mrs Brook who was also feeling bereft of Vince's bright presence and gentle teasing. She looked shocked.

'What an idea, Inspector sir. Why, there are your two wee girls growing up in Orkney. In a few years they will be ready to come to Edinburgh and do their duty by their papa.' And with one of her sly looks, she added coyly, 'That is, if there isn't a second Mrs Faro by then.'

Ignoring his gesture of impatient dismissal, she went on, 'I do hope and pray to the good Lord every night that you will meet a nice lady of your own age some day, that I do, Inspector sir.'

Faro's disapproving sniff was the answer she expected. Any argument that he put forward would be totally ignored. From long experience he knew that dignified silence was the only weapon against romantically inclined females of a certain age. They should have known better, but persisted in regarding marriage as the rose-strewn path to 'happy-ever-after-land'.

His mother and Mrs Brook were of one mind on the subject. But apart from occasional yearnings for a mate to share his bed and some of his dreams, Faro felt that the harmonious bachelor life had much to commend it and suited him well. The many daily hazards in a policeman's life made for poor husband material and he still suffered pangs of remorse recalling his neglect of poor Lizzie who had never once reproached him.

'As long as I have the bairns, dear, I am never lonely.' But the son they had both longed for after two daughters, had killed her.

At least Rose and Emily, with the resilience of childhood, were now settling happily and healthily with their grandmother while his stepson, after completing his year as Dr Kellar's assistant, would open the ground floor of 9 Sheridan Place as the surgery and consulting rooms of Dr Vincent Beaumarcher Laurie, general practitioner of medicine.

But without Vince's presence, Faro could hardly bear the Sunday afternoon ritual of tending the little grave in Greyfriars Kirkyard where Lizzie lay asleep with their baby at her side. He could still sob out loud at that bitter remembrance.

Once, unbearably alone, he had thought to love again and he carefully avoided the pathway by the willow tree, haunted by memories of his first meeting with the beautiful actress he had dreamed so passionately and so fleetingly, of making his wife.*

Never, never again, he swore. Let others fall in love and marry. It was not for him.

On the day he expected Vince's return from Vienna, Faro arrived at the Central Office as usual, to learn that

* *Enter Second Murderer*

his presence was being eagerly sought by Superintendent McIntosh.

'Close the door and sit down, Faro. I have a rather delicate task for you, one which must be handled with the utmost confidence and care.' He shook his head sternly. 'Should information leak out of this office and the general public hear about it . . . '

'What is this task, sir?' asked Faro somewhat impatiently. McIntosh's normal instructions regarding his senior detective inspector's apprehension of criminals came down rather heavily on the side of brutal methods. Gentle persuasion was an art unknown to the tough Superintendent.

'Something very serious has happened. Something which, I need not tell you, might have the most serious repercussions on the reputation of our police establishment. It concerns Dr Kellar's wife.' McIntosh paused dramatically. 'She has disappeared.'

'Disappeared, sir? When did this happen?'

'About two weeks ago. They had a dinner party for a few friends.'

'Yes, Superintendent. I know. I was there.'

McIntosh's head shot up and he regarded Faro with some astonishment. 'Why, of course you were, of course. Well, well, that does help.'

'Help? In what way?'

'The very next morning it appears that Mrs Kellar left to go on a visit to her sister at North Berwick. Dr Kellar dropped her at Waverley railway station. She had sent a wire to her sister to expect her off the 12.45 train. When she didn't arrive, Mrs Findlay-Cupar wasn't unduly alarmed at first. She expected her the next day, but after two more days when Mrs Kellar still hadn't put in an appearance nor sent any explanation, her sister despatched a letter asking what had happened.

'As this was addressed to Mrs Kellar personally, the housekeeper, who is new, didn't regard it as urgent. Dr Kellar had told her the mistress was only away for a day or two, so she put it with other letters for Mrs Kellar on her writing desk, where it lay unread. An unfortunate set of circumstances, you'll agree. It was not until another week had passed without any word from Mrs Kellar indicating when she was returning home that Dr Kellar, glancing through her letters, opened the one from his sister-in-law. He immediately set out for North Berwick.'

Leaning back in his chair, McIntosh studied Faro's expression. 'Well, have you any explanation?'

Faro shrugged. Had he not been witness to the events at the Kellars' dinner party, his sense of danger would have been alerted and he would have viewed this disappearance with more alarm. He said as much to the Superintendent.

'You were present, sir.' Guessing at the unevenness of McIntosh's domestic bliss and harmony with The Tartar, he found it irresistible not to add, 'Surely the answer is obvious to a married man, sir?'

'Not to me, it isn't,' said McIntosh, eyeing him sternly.

'I would imagine that Mrs Kellar is teaching her husband a lesson.'

'A lesson, Inspector? What kind of lesson?'

'I think we'll discover that Mrs Kellar has left home and taken refuge with an understanding friend or relative, giving Dr Kellar time to regret his disagreeable conduct in front of their guests.'

'Yes, yes, Inspector. Maybe so. But where the devil is she?'

'She doubtless intends that to be kept secret meantime. Especially from her husband.'

'So that's what you believe?' Stroking his beard thoughtfully, McIntosh stared at Faro. 'All part of making Dr Kellar suffer, eh. I'm not saying I disagree with you entirely, but the doctor is a very worried man and expects us to do something about finding his missing wife. What you are suggesting has obviously never occurred to him.'

McIntosh added a sudden bark of laughter, as if the idea pleased him. 'Scandal, that's at the back of it. A breath of scandal would ruin his chance of the knighthood. He insists that discreet enquiries begin immediately. I'm afraid that whatever the outcome, even if we all end up looking like idiots and Mrs Kellar walks in tomorrow, we'll have to humour him.'

'Very well, Superintendent. I'll proceed along the normal missing person lines and interview Dr Kellar first. I imagine he's checked the hospitals and so forth?'

'The first place he'd look, Faro,' said McIntosh sternly.

'Very well. I'll get confirmation of what he told you—'

'No need for that, Faro,' McIntosh interrupted hastily. 'He's told me all he knows and I've imparted the information to you. That's enough. He won't take kindly to being questioned again so you'd better talk to the servants. For heaven's sake, choose a time during the day when he's not at home. Then a visit to Mrs Findlay-Cupar.' He handed over a scrap of paper. 'Her address in North Berwick. Another person who might know something is the Mad – er, Sir Hedley.'

'I'd already thought of that. Solomon's Tower would be a good place to seek refuge.'

'As long as she likes cats. And what about that friend of hers, the young widow?'

'Mrs Shaw?'

'They seemed very friendly.'

'Very well. I'll try Regent Crescent.'

McIntosh frowned. 'But only see this Mrs Shaw if all other enquiries lead nowhere. Dr Kellar made quite a point about insisting on absolute discretion. So better keep it in the family.'

Taking the Superintendent's advice, Faro decided that Kellar was at this moment likely to be found giving his morning lecture at Surgeons Hall, demonstrating the arts of carving up corpses to a group of admiring students with strong stomachs.

Vince had told him that this ordeal was frequently too harrowing. Dazzling on the playing field, prepared to carry their medical knowledge for Queen and country to battlefield or to darkest Africa, sturdy young men frequently dropped like ninepins and had to be gathered up from the floor and revived with smelling salts.

If Kellar suffered from a sense of humour, then it was of the macabre variety. He allocated to students with the weakest stomachs the most gruesome tasks related to the human corpse, relishing their discomfort and distress.

Faro left the horse-drawn omnibus which took him part of the way. It was a freezing day, and he walked rapidly in the direction of the police surgeon's house in the Grange. The snow by the roadside had melted and refrozen several times during the last week. It lay grey and pitted and his boots slipped ominously as he tried to avoid every passing vehicle which threw up a fountain of disagreeable brown slush.

The drive down to the Kellar house was hardly less hazardous under foot but mercifully without any traffic. At this hour servants should have been busily engaged in their household tasks but ten minutes later, as he waited on the front steps and the bell pealed through the house unattended, he wondered if his errand had been in vain.

His third summons brought forth a tiny housemaid who looked all of twelve years old, frail and undernourished, with what his Orkney mother called 'not a picking on her bones' and the hugest palest eyes he had ever seen.

'Detective Inspector Faro, to see Mrs Flynn, if you please.'

The girl's eyes grew wider, almost colourless, the pupils reduced to tiny black points. She regarded him with apprehension and he felt a desperate need to put this frightened child at her ease.

He gave her a warm and friendly smile. 'What's your name, lass?'

'Ina, sir.' The words were whispered with a slight shuddering movement away from him, as if the response to her name encouraged a violent reaction. She would see if Mrs Flynn was in.

Pitifully thin and frail, in a skirt several sizes too large for her, she seemed to float rather than scuttle across the hall to disappear in the direction of the downstairs kitchen. Her extreme youth was in keeping with Kellar's policy of employing child labour since it was cheap, thought Faro grimly. It was a disgrace. Thank God there were women like Mrs Kellar with her kind heart who allowed such lasses the privilege of returning to their homes at weekends.

Ina reappeared promptly and this time remembered to bob a respectful curtsey to the gentleman. 'Mrs Flynn will see you directly, sir.'

He followed her across the handsome panelled hall lit by many Gothic windows where a door disguised as an antique cupboard gave access down a steep flight of stairs into a gloomy basement, whose only light seemed to be reflected from whitewashed stone walls. Cold as the day was outside, he suspected sunshine seldom penetrated these dank nether regions. What a contrast from the handsome house above. These dismal stone-flagged floors and rough-hewn walled quarters, with every window barred, gave the illusion less of a house than a prison.

Faro knew all about such matters from Lizzie. She had told him that the reason for the barred windows was not only to keep intruders out, but equally important, to keep skittish and flighty maids and their followers from making easy exits and entrances at all hours. Once the master or the trusted housekeeper bearing her iron ring of keys had secured and bolted the doors at ten thirty each night, the servants were virtually prisoners until next day. Morning roll-call, as breakfast prayers were called in large houses, for those who had found themselves locked out the night before, brought retribution in the form of instant dismissal. For a servant girl innocently delayed, perhaps by visiting a sick relative, the future was bleak indeed, unless she was pretty enough to be taken on without references. If she was plain and had dependants, often the only answer to starvation was prostitution. Manservants fared somewhat better. In the ever-growing labouring class, cheap work and strong bodies were called for and no questions asked or references required.

Faro was not altogether surprised to find the housekeeper installed in a room poorly furnished and lit by the stumps of two feeble candles. She poked a few miserable coals into a lot of smoke without attendant fire and apologised that her bag of coal was finished. She was not due another until next week. Her bulky frame huddled in a thick shawl, the inevitable scarf about her neck, she grumbled hoarsely.

'If the mistress had been here she would have seen me right. But it's no good asking *him*. I keep out of *his* way as much as I can.'

Faro could well believe it as he nodded sympathetically and edged his chair closer to the fireplace. Really, the atmosphere was colder here indoors than it was outside, for this basement added a clammy dampness to the chill. He would have thought twice about keeping a pet dog or the Sheridan Place cat Rusty in such conditions and felt a surge of righteous indignation towards Kellar whose meanness bordered on cruelty to his servants.

Mrs Flynn managed to lower her chin back into the warm protection of the scarf.

'I trust your toothache—' Faro began.

'Better, sir. The gumboil burst. Only I got this awful sore throat,' she said, patting the scarf. 'Hurts to talk.'

'I'm sorry. Shall I come back?'

'No, no. I'll manage. Is it something urgent – about the mistress?' she asked eagerly.

'I wondered if you could help us with our enquiries, if you had any ideas where she might have gone. You know, friends and so forth.'

Mrs Flynn shook her head. 'She's left him. I'm sure of that.'

'So one would suppose.'

'Run away from him, that's what. And about time. And good luck to her. That's what I say,' she added defiantly.

'Yes, Mrs Flynn, but this is just speculation. Unless you have any proof? Did she tell you, or give any hint, that running away was her intention?'

'I'm not sure what you mean, sir?'

'Well, did she indicate that she might be gone for some time?'

'No.'

'She didn't leave you any instructions?'

'No, sir.'

'Wasn't that rather odd?'

'She probably didn't think it was worthwhile as I'm working my notice.' Mrs Flynn thought for a moment and then added, 'But I knew something was wrong. I saw how upset she was the night before, helping me in the kitchen. I tried not to notice, but she was crying her eyes out, the poor love.'

'Are you a married woman, Mrs Flynn?'

'A widow. For more than twenty years. I see what you're getting at, Inspector. All married folks quarrel a bit and don't I know it, as a housekeeper.' She laughed harshly. 'But Mrs Kellar was different. She doted on the master, anyone could see that with half an eye.'

She let this information sink in for a moment and then added, 'Besides she must have run away, otherwise she would have been at North Berwick, wouldn't she?'

'What happened exactly that last morning?'

'Ina came in early and took the wire from the mistress to the post office.'

'Did you see it?'

'Oh yes. It said, "Arriving today off 12.45 train from Edinburgh." I was making soup when the mistress shouted down that she was leaving. When I came upstairs, I saw the doctor handing her into the carriage.'

Mrs Flynn paused to lean over and retrieve a coal from the feeble fire. 'I opened the door and overheard a bit of an argument. It was snowing quite hard and he was shouting at her: "Get in. Get in, woman. I'll take you there, the blasted station or all the way, if I have to."'

'You're quite sure that's what he said?'

'I'd swear to it in a court of law, Inspector,' said Mrs Flynn firmly. 'The blasted station or all the way,' she repeated, watching Faro make a note of the words.

'So he was driving her himself. No coachman?'

Mrs Flynn chuckled. 'There was not. Him? Waste money on a coachman? Oh, I hear that he sometimes gets a fellow from the hiring place down the road, but only for special occasions. Says he likes driving himself.'

'When did you see the doctor again that day?'

Mrs Flynn frowned. 'I didn't, sir.'

'He didn't return directly from the station?'

'I'm not sure but I don't think so.'

'What about meals? Didn't you serve him supper?'

The housekeeper shook her head. 'No, he hadn't left any note on the hall table that morning. That's the usual procedure. We have strict instructions, if there's no note saying what he wants to eat, then we are to presume he wishes to remain undisturbed or he's dining at his club.'

'When did you see him again, then?'

'Not until later that week at supper time. I can't remember which day it was.'

'He didn't seem anxious or upset in any way by Mrs Kellar's absence?'

'Of course not. Why should he? He had no idea that she had gone for good until he opened that letter from her sister.'

'And then, how did he behave?'

'Behave, sir?' Mrs Flynn thought for a moment. 'I didn't see him reading it. He just rang the bell for me and when I went upstairs he was sitting with a letter in his hand. "I have to go to North Berwick immediately." That was all he said.'

'Did he look shocked?'

'I couldn't say, sir. He had his back to me. Never looks at us, or speaks to us directly, if it can be avoided. So I guessed something serious had happened. I asked him if the mistress was ill and he snapped my head off. "None of your business, Flynn." I asked him if he was going to be away long, and reminded him that I was working my notice and would be leaving on Saturday. He said, did I have a situation to go to, and when I said no, he said then I'd better stay on meantime until the mistress came back.'

The housekeeper leaned back in her chair and sighed deeply, as if exhausted by the toll of this lengthy explanation on her sore throat.

Faro got to his feet. 'Thank you, Mrs Flynn, you have been most helpful. I wonder if I might ask you one other favour.'

Mrs Flynn stirred from her reverie. 'Yes, sir, of course.'

'You saw Mrs Kellar leaving? Did she take much luggage?'

'A leather travelling bag. Smallish. I carried it downstairs.'

'Did you help her pack?'

'No, I'm not a personal maid, sir. She wouldn't expect me to do that for her, although I did repair a petticoat hem that was torn, as an obligement.'

'What was she wearing, by the way?'

'Her lovely fur cloak, sable or something like that. Black with a shoulder cape. And a dark green costume with brown braid, a cream-coloured silk blouse. Looked a picture, she did. Is there anything else, sir?'

'I wonder if I could have a look at her room.'

'Her room, sir. Which one would you be meaning? Him and her both had their own bedrooms.'

'I'd like to see the room she occupied.'

'I don't see why not. Ina will show you.'

The housekeeper rang the handbell on her table and Faro asked, 'By the way, could you let me have a list of any callers Mrs Kellar received during the days before she left?'

'Callers?' Mrs Flynn frowned. 'You mean tradesmen and the like?'

'I was thinking of more personal callers.'

Mrs Flynn gave a throaty chuckle. 'Oh, you mean gentleman callers and such, do you, Inspector?'

Faro tried to look nonchalant. 'Something like that.'

'Only the young doctor, him that works for the master. He was with you at the dinner party. He calls on Mrs Kellar quite regularly. He looked in as she was packing. Went upstairs and stayed for . . . ' Mrs Flynn paused and thought, 'for twenty minutes or so. I expect his address will be in her book up on the writing desk, if you want it.'

She obviously had no idea that Vince was his stepson. A tap on the door announced Ina and, turning to leave, Faro said, 'One thing more, Mrs Flynn. Is there anything missing from the house that Mrs Kellar might have taken with her besides her personal possessions?'

Mrs Flynn gave him a puzzled look. 'I couldn't say, sir. I'm new to this house. It takes years to get to know one well.'

'Well, if you hear of anything missing, you will let me know.'

Glad to be out of the housekeeper's gloomy uncomfortable sitting-room, Faro thanked her for her help and followed Ina along the chilly corridor and into the hall, to gratefully breathe in the purer air of the house's upper regions.

As they climbed the stairs, he asked, 'Did you assist the mistress to pack?'

'No, sir. She didn't ask.'

Ina opened the door into a bedroom expensively furnished, but apart from the silver brushes, jewel box and toilette set on the dressing table, there were fewer mementoes than Faro would have expected to see. This characterless room gave no hints about Mrs Kellar's personality, but he realised that he could hardly, with decorum and in the presence of the maid, conduct a careful search of wardrobe and chest of drawers.

'Do you come into this room every day?'

'Yes, sir. I make up the bed and clear the ashes from the fire, re-lay it. I empty the slops and dust . . . '

'Good. Then you can tell me if anything has been moved since Mrs Kellar left.'

'Nothing, sir. Mrs Kellar is a very neat tidy lady, very thoughtful for everyone.'

'She didn't have a personal maid?'

'Oh no, sir. The master didn't think such expense was justified and Mrs Flynn told me that when the mistress's maid who had been with her for years took sick and left, he said a housekeeper and a maid should be enough.'

'Do you happen to know where Mrs Kellar's maid lives?'

'She died last year and Mrs Kellar went to her funeral. Such a kind lady, if it wasn't for her, he'd never get anyone to stay. Look at Mrs Flynn. She's only staying on as a favour – he had to fair beg her, I'll bet. And now she's working her notice, so to speak, she's very hoity-toity.'

Suspecting compassion from this nice policeman, Ina was no longer bashful or afraid. 'She does as little as possible, I can tell you. Says she's poorly with her toothache and her sore throat, gives me my orders, prepares the doctor's dinner and then retires to her room . . . '

Only half-listening to this tirade against Mrs Flynn, Faro was surveying the room very carefully, making mental pictures of the contents. When he left he would be able to write out an exact list of everything it contained. That was part of his job.

The writing desk by the window was a handsome davenport. He opened the lid and a cursory glance revealed the usual stationery and pens. There was no address book in evidence. It might have been pushed into a drawer but, in all probability, Mrs Kellar had taken it with her.

Looking around, he concluded there was not the slightest

indication in this peaceful, strangely impersonal room that Mabel Kellar had intended anything other than to spend a few days visiting her sister.

Where was she then? What had he overlooked?

His attention kept returning to that dressing table. He touched the silver brushes with a strange feeling that there was a lot more in Mabel Kellar's disappearance than he had first thought. Now he wondered whether the answer lay deeper and wider than a long-suffering wife teaching her ungrateful husband a lesson by leaving him to the tender mercies of incompetent servants.

'Will that be all, sir?'

Faro nodded and followed the maid on to the landing. He pointed to the drawing-room: 'May I?'

Crossing the floor, he opened the double doors leading into the dining-room. Sterile without the softening effects of candlelight, an atmosphere of melancholy pervaded the long table with chairs devoid of diners. He was not surprised to hear that Dr Kellar did not have his meals there.

'When the mistress isn't at home, he eats in his study across the way.'

Faro strode towards the study door. At present, Kellar's wife was merely missing from home and he had merely requested exhaustive enquiries to be made. He could imagine the doctor's righteous indignation, which would surely rebound on Detective Inspector Faro's head personally, should he return home unexpectedly. But the opportunity was too good to miss.

'Oh sir, you can't go in there. No one's allowed. He always keeps it locked.'

A pity. Kellar's study could well be the only room in the house where confidential information as to why his wife had left him might be found. But without authority, Faro was treading on very delicate ground. And without positive evidence that a crime had been committed he could hardly proceed to search the police surgeon's house.

'No matter. You have been most helpful, Ina.'

At the top of the stairs, the maid paused. 'There is something, sir.' Again she hesitated. 'I overheard you asking Mrs Flynn if there was anything missing.'

'Well, is there?'

Ina played nervously with the starched edge of her apron. 'I didn't want to mention it in front of Mrs Flynn, or I'll be blamed. You see, she hasn't noticed so far, but when the doctor finds out . . . ' She looked up at him with huge scared eyes. 'One of his precious carving knives has gone.'

'When did you discover this?'

'When I was washing up after the dinner party, that morning the mistress left. I was putting everything back and I suddenly noticed when I went upstairs to put the special silver back in the canteen that there was only one carving knife. I've searched for the other, but it's never turned up. I just can't find it anywhere.'

As she spoke she led the way back into the dining-room and walked over to the mahogany sideboard.

'There, sir.' She watched eagerly as Faro opened the elegant velvet-lined case, as if his action might miraculously restore the missing knife to its embossed silver-handled partner.

'Mrs Flynn will skin me alive when she finds out.'

'Oh come now, lass. I shouldn't worry too much. It'll turn up, you'll see. Probably put into the wrong drawer.'

But Ina was shaking her head. 'No, sir. It's not that. I know, I just know, that something – something wicked has happened to it.'

'Wicked?' Faro laughed uneasily.

'Yes, sir. Wicked.' The huge eyes turned on him again, almost tearfully this time. 'I see things, sir. People laugh at me, but I can't help it. There's something black, black and wicked going on in this house. I know it. Come the weekend, the master'll go mad. He'll never carve the roast . . . '

Faro was no longer listening. 'By the pricking of my

thumbs, something wicked this way comes.' Shakespeare, who belonged in a very different world to this simple maid, had been aware of the same devils. And so was Faro, his senses warning him of the enormity of the girl's words. Worse, he had a sudden inescapable vision of Vince saying, 'I could have snatched up one of those knives and plunged it into his black heart.'

Only this time, perhaps the missing knife had been plunged into everyone's favourite, Mabel Kellar.

Chapter Four

A great believer in the thought-clarifying powers of fresh air, on leaving the Kellar house Faro decided to walk around the extensive gardens. A gratifying burst of sunshine had temporarily demolished the leaden skies, turning untrodden snow and delicately frosted hedgerows into a semblance of winter fairyland. There was warmth on the sheltered paths and above his head birds twittered in a hopeful prelude to spring.

He breathed deeply, enjoying this blissful moment between the acts of winter's cruel drama, for he had little doubt that the heavy skies above the Pentland Hills foretold yet another snowfall was imminent.

How was Vince faring, he wondered, delighted that the lad would soon be home again. It had seemed a curious time to choose for a brief holiday at an asylum for consumptives in the Austrian Alps. One of the resident doctors had been Vince's close friend during University days and, Faro remembered, Walter had a very pretty sister.

He leaned against a tree in the sun and lit a pipe. Surrounded by so much beauty, the subtle varied shades of umber and heliotrope and rose, he could never understand why people thought of winter as being the drab dead time of year.

Looking across at the house, for the first time he envied the lot of those who could live in such comfort and enjoy splendid gardens of their own, akin to a small park. If he ever retired from the Police, or escaped the hazards of grievous bodily harm that threatened him almost daily, then he would crave a tiny house with a garden.

Suddenly the years ahead seemed very bleak. His ancestors had been Orkney crofters, perhaps their blood unsettled him from time to time. Why had he chosen this violent, unpredictable life of fighting criminals? Had it begun originally in order to avenge his policeman father who had been murdered for getting too close to the truth?*

Whatever his reason, it was too late to go back now and he was once more committed to solving yet another of those baffling mysteries that were his daily bread, of trying to get inside the criminal's head and walk around in his skin for a while, in an effort to piece together motives and opportunities. In this case, however, he suspected that there was no evidence of any kind beyond a domestic tiff.

The vital question remained. Was Kellar making too much of his missing wife? Had she merely absconded to teach her husband a lesson? Did he suspect that too?

Faro smiled grimly. Anyone less important than the police surgeon would have received a rude reception, told by Superintendent McIntosh not to be so daft and waste his precious time sending his senior Detective Inspector off on a wild goose chase. Walking towards the gates, he would have been inclined to agree except that his visit to the Kellar home had left some disquieting observations to mull over on his return to the Central Office.

First, the missing carving knife. Since cutlery had a habit of being mislaid or misappropriated in the best of houses, there was perhaps a perfectly innocent explanation. Mrs Flynn, uncertain of where everything was kept, had slipped it into the wrong drawer. But Ina, who was responsible for the washing up and stowing away of dishes had seemed so sure.

Faro would have liked to discuss the matter with Mrs Flynn but a tactful approach was needed, one that wouldn't involve getting Ina into trouble with her employer. Dr

* *Blood Line*

Kellar's displeasure, rebounding on the housekeeper would, in the pecking order of such establishments, descend upon the hapless maid as everyone's scapegoat.

Why did that carving knife bother him? Was it because he kept on hearing Vince's words about plunging it into Kellar's black heart for his treatment of Mabel?

Faro was glad his stepson had been out of the country when she disappeared. He didn't care for the idea of Vince being associated, however remotely, with the police surgeon's absconding wife. In what must inevitably become known in Edinburgh circles as 'the Kellar scandal', even the innocent friendship of a very young man and a misunderstood middle-aged wife would be seized upon eagerly as a tantalising morsel of delicious gossip.

Yet even more disquieting than the missing carving knife was the picture that persisted of Mrs Kellar's bedroom and the feeling that there was something important he had overlooked. Deep in thought, Faro had almost reached the gates when a brougham approached. The familiar face of Dr Kellar leaned down from the driving seat, and Faro cursed under his breath, wishing he had made his escape two minutes earlier.

'Looking for me by any chance, Inspector?'

Pocketing his pipe, Faro nodded vaguely.

'I thought you might be paying me a visit, despite McIntosh being in possession of all the facts.' And tapping the Inspector's shoulder with his whip, Kellar said, 'No need to apologise. I haven't worked with the City Police for years without knowing all about the keen noses of detectives. In search of clues they could, and frequently do, put bloodhounds to shame. Have to visit the scene of the crime and all that sort of thing.'

'We don't know that a crime has been committed, sir,' said Faro sharply.

Kellar was unperturbed. 'A mere slip of the tongue – a figure of speech. I should have called it "the last known sighting".' His laugh was light hearted, causing

Faro to study him intently. If this was a guilty man, then he was behaving with considerably more aplomb than one might have presumed normal in the circumstances.

'Well, what are you waiting for, man?' Kellar indicated the seat alongside. 'Climb up. Come along to the house. Search the place to your heart's content.'

'At present we are merely investigating a disappearance, sir. Proceeding along the usual lines, beginning with relatives—'

'You are wasting your time. Her sister and her uncle know nothing,' Kellar interrupted.

'Then there are the hospitals.'

'Hospitals?'

'You will have already consulted their recent admissions lists?'

'Of course not. Why should I? What on earth for?' was the indignant reply.

Faro looked at him sternly. 'Suppose Mrs Kellar has been injured and has lost her memory. Or had an accident and was pushed from the train. Surely such possibilities have occurred to you?'

'What nonsense. Absolute rubbish,' roared Kellar.

Faro thought for a moment before replying. 'Then you believe that your wife is unharmed and that her disappearance is deliberate.' When Kellar stared at him blankly, he continued, 'If that is so, Dr Kellar, then you realise that you are putting a great strain on a police force already overburdened and that your action is hampering the investigation of serious crimes.'

'I am merely taking precautions I deem necessary, Inspector Faro,' shouted Kellar, pointing again to the carriage seat. 'Come along. Search my house. I have nothing to hide.'

Tempted, Faro hesitated and Kellar smiled grimly. 'Ah, I see I'm too late and that you've searched already. Find anything interesting that I should know about?'

'A search of the premises is hardly necessary. Or proper, sir. Not at the moment,' Faro reminded him.

'Not at the moment,' Kellar seized upon the words and repeated them slowly. 'Now that does sound ominous.'

Suddenly anxious, he leaned over staring down into Faro's face. 'Surely – surely to God, I'm not under suspicion. You can't think I – I – ?' Words failed him and observing with growing horror Faro's stern expression, he shouted, 'That is absolutely ludicrous, Inspector. I yelled at her, and in company, as you are aware. But then I do so frequently and she has never seized upon this as an excuse to leave me.'

When Faro didn't reply, he said angrily, 'I don't like your suspicious look, Inspector, indeed I do not. It offends me deeply.' And thumping the whip against the seat, 'My God, this is beyond a joke. I thought I had convinced McIntosh that there was a perfectly natural explanation for my wife behaving as she did and she will return home eventually.'

'Then why did you insist on an enquiry, sir?'

'Oh, I don't know. To teach her a lesson. I was confused and angry. I thought it was my duty to regard the matter as one that should be investigated – discreetly – just in case she had met with an accident – then my tardiness would pose a question in some quarters—'

'Then tell me, sir,' Faro interrupted. 'Why are you objecting to our enquiries? Had you some suspicions of your own regarding her whereabouts which you haven't imparted to Superintendent McIntosh?'

'What kind of suspicions?' Kellar demanded.

'Well, let us say, you suspected that your wife's destination was not North Berwick with her sister. That she perhaps had some other – well, assignation.'

Kellar stared at him. 'I haven't the least idea what you mean. What the devil are you implying, Faro?'

Faro sighed. 'To put it delicately, sir, was there any possibility that there was some other man involved.'

'You mean a lover. My Mabel?' Kellar's head shot back,

his mouth open in a roar of mirth. Then suddenly sober, he leaned over, his face inches away from Faro's. 'My wife worships the ground I walk on. There never was and never will be another man for her.'

And so, since time began, has every cuckolded husband believed, thought Faro grimly.

'Get this into your head, Faro. I've told you all the reasons why I mentioned her disappearance. But between ourselves, I haven't the slightest doubt that once she has come to her senses and realised that this is a joke in very poor taste, she will come back to me.'

So that was it and Faro felt sudden anger. A discreet private investigation, McIntosh had called it. None of the usual sources which would bring Kellar into the public gaze. Not out of natural caring and anxiety for his wife – oh no. Kellar probably didn't give a damn whether she had gone or not, but his lack of interest might be misinterpreted. A blot on his reputation as a devoted husband, a model citizen, and there might be second thoughts about the knighthood.

Faro regarded him with ill-concealed distaste. He had had quite enough of Dr Kellar. 'I trust your assumptions are correct, sir. Now if you'll excuse me.'

Back at the Central Office, Superintendent McIntosh was eagerly awaiting Faro's arrival.

Ushering him into the office, McIntosh closed the door. 'Look at this, Faro.' On a side table were the remains of a parcel of large dimensions, its brown paper wrapping disintegrating, sodden and wet.

Slowly the Superintendent drew out what appeared at first glance to be the limp remains of a dead animal, its fur sticky with mud. Watching Faro's face, he lifted it carefully and shook out the folds to reveal a fur cloak, a once-treasured possession, soft as a caress, cared for as the most exquisite and valuable garment in any well-to-do woman's wardrobe. The fur was sable with a black cape. Its ruin was not mud as Faro had first thought. A closer look was enough to reveal that it had been soaked in blood.

'Where . . . ?'

'Just brought in, Faro,' said McIntosh excitedly. 'Found beside the railway line near Longniddry Station. May have lain under the snow for a while. The railwayman who handed it in happened to notice that the melting snow had turned pink. He thought at first it was a dead cat.' Touching an area of the fur less bloodied, McIntosh added, 'Looks expensive, doesn't it. Not the sort of thing one would throw away without good reason. Any ideas, Faro?'

'One or two, sir. I think you'll find that it belongs to Mrs Kellar.'

'Mrs Kellar!' McIntosh gave a yelp of astonishment. 'Mrs Kellar! How do you know that?'

'Because I've just been to the Kellar house and this answers exactly the description of what she was wearing when she left the house for North Berwick.'

'You're sure?'

Faro examined the furrier's label. There weren't many who could afford such a couturier. 'Tracing the owner shouldn't present any difficulties and I think we'll find that was specially made for Mrs Kellar.'

McIntosh sat back in his chair and rubbed his hands together. 'Well now, if you're right, that's an extraordinary stroke of luck.'

Faro gave him a sharp glance, surprised by his insensitivity. Whoever had last worn this cloak – and if his assumptions were correct the last wearer had been Mrs Kellar – had run seriously out of luck.

'The railwayman thought it might have fallen out of a passing train.'

'More likely to have been thrown out,' said Faro.

'Well, whichever, it's been hidden by the snow.' McIntosh thought for a moment. 'If it belongs to Mrs Kellar then it could have lain there since she disappeared. Nice piece of fur. I suppose we were lucky to have it handed in at all.'

Faro was turning the cloak inside out. 'Extensive staining here too. Look at the lining.'

'No doubt that was the real reason for the person who found it not being keen to keep it.'

'All we need is the weapon . . . '

'Oh, I think we have that too,' said McIntosh with a grin, and from under the brown paper, with the air of a magician producing a rabbit from a hat, he dramatically withdrew a large knife. 'This was wrapped inside the fur.'

Faro held out his hand for the knife. Without a second's hesitation, he said, 'These are undoubtedly bloodstains.'

The information slowly dawned on the Superintendent. 'My God, Faro,' he whispered, 'you realise what you're saying. Someone murdered the police surgeon's wife. There'll be all hell to pay over this. If we can only find where this knife came from,' he added.

'Oh, I can tell you that too.'

'You can?'

Faro nodded. 'Yes. As a matter of fact, we've both seen the murder weapon before and fairly recently.'

McIntosh stared at him. 'We have?'

'Oh yes, and fairly recently. At Dr Kellar's dinner party the night before his wife vanished.'

Faro studied his superior's horrified expression with the grim satisfaction of knowing, without the least doubt, that what he held in his hand was one of a pair missing from the dining-room which had been used to more gruesome purpose than the carving of a ruined lamb roast.

Chapter Five

Superintendent McIntosh was put out of countenance by the enormity of the discovery of the fur cloak and the carving knife. Only a half-wit could now presume they were searching for an absconding wife when all the evidence pointed indisputably to the fact that Mabel Kellar had not only disappeared, but had been foully murdered.

Worse, suspicion might now be reasonably directed to the personal involvement in the crime of Edinburgh City Police's surgeon. Fearful repercussions were anticipated by the Superintendent when this disclosure was made public. Such circumstances demanded that Dr Kellar be confronted, on what McIntosh called neutral territory, to give a good account of himself, if that were humanly possible.

'Tactfully, you understand, Faro. Very tactfully. You can talk around it, you know the procedure well enough,' he said hurriedly, as was his way when he wished to rid himself of an unpleasant duty. 'See if he has any ideas about how his wife's bloodstained fur came to be found on the railway line.'

Faro smiled grimly at this somewhat naive method of approach. The evidence was overwhelming and had it been any other suspect than Kellar, doubtless policemen and the jail coach would already be bowling towards Surgeons Hall. Led by Detective Inspector Faro, the doctor would be questioned and if there were no satisfactory answers, then a warrant would be presented for apprehension on suspicion of murder. Considering the importance of the suspect and his unique role with Edinburgh City Police, Superintendent McIntosh seized his greatcoat and, more grim-faced than usual, decided to accompany his Inspector and be present at the interview.

A carriage bore both men rapidly towards Surgeons Hall. They travelled in silence as the thought hung unspoken and uneasily in their minds that they were already too late. Dr Kellar, aware of the damning discovery at Longniddry, might well have taken prudent flight.

It was almost with surprise that they met him emerging from the lecture hall. He did not seem in the least concerned at this unexpected visit.

'Is there somewhere we can talk, sir?' asked Faro.

'In private, if you please, doctor,' added McIntosh sternly.

Kellar nodded and opened the door into a rather dark study with all the comforting atmosphere of a bleak and draughty station waiting-room on a cold winter's day.

Motioning Faro and McIntosh towards two woefully uncomfortable wooden chairs, he perched on the edge of the table and for the first time he seemed to notice the parcel under Faro's arm, now re-wrapped in fresh brown paper. Sighing, he said heavily, 'Well,gentlemen, I suppose it's about Mabel, isn't it?'

Faro looked at him in amazement. Did he already know what the parcel contained and, if so, was he about to confess? If he did, this would be one of the most remarkable cases on record, with very little detection involved: confession upon confrontation before any accusation could be made. Such a situation was not unknown, especially in a case of crime passionel, but Faro had expected the police surgeon to be made of stronger stuff, to be wily and evasive.

Dr Kellar stabbed a finger in his direction. 'Go on, Faro, out with it.'

Faro noted the uncertainty. He had been mistaken about the confession and said, somewhat awkwardly, 'Thank you, sir.' This was not an interview that he relished.

'God knows what I expected,' he told Vince later. 'Sobs and screams of rage. When you consider how he could take on about a burnt roast and yet the same man could receive with complete aplomb the almost positive proof that his wife had, in all probability, been dismembered with the same carving knife he had used that Sunday evening.'

Faro was aware that the Superintendent was also watching Kellar's expression intently as he unwrapped the parcel and shook forth the bloodstained cloak and knife.

A faint groan hissed out of Kellar, his visible signs of discomfort were that his face paled, his knuckles whitening as he gripped the edge of the table.

He made no attempt to touch the stained fur which Faro spread before him. 'I want to see the label,' he demanded. When this was revealed, he nodded. 'Yes, there's no doubt about it. It belongs to Mabel. The knife?' He shook his head. 'It is not unique. I believe you would find one exactly like that, in my dining-room.'

'I'm afraid, sir, we have no option but to treat your wife's disappearance as a murder investigation,' said the Superintendent, clearing his throat in some embarrassment.

Kellar nodded rapidly, almost eagerly. 'Quite right, Superintendent. Quite right. If you will excuse me for a moment.' He put his hand to his mouth and gulped. 'I think I am about to be sick.'

He left the room hastily, while McIntosh and Faro exchanged uncomfortable glances. They avoided looking towards the revolting and incriminating evidence as each meditated on what the next move should be when Kellar returned.

'Perhaps you should have gone with him, Faro,' whispered McIntosh with a quick glance at the clock, and leaving the Inspector to wonder if at this moment Kellar was making a run for it.

Pretending to misunderstand, Faro said, 'I don't think

that would be strictly necessary.' Walking over to the fireplace empty of anything capable of ignition, he leaned on the stone mantel and concentrated on some particularly uninspired watercolours. 'A gentleman who is being sick prefers to be private.'

McIntosh came and stared curiously over Faro's shoulder as if he had discovered a lost Rembrandt. 'Interesting, eh?'

The door opened at that moment and thankfully they beheld Kellar, somewhat green about the gills, dabbing at his beard with a silk handkerchief. 'Please be seated, gentlemen.' He looked round the room, and said shakily, 'I should like to sit down myself, if you don't mind.'

Faro indicated the chair he had vacated.

'Thank you, Inspector. Ah, that's better. Now, perhaps we could all do with a dram. The cupboard over there, Faro, if you wouldn't mind doing the honours.'

The cupboard smelt of mould and mice but the glasses and decanter were a welcome sight and the whisky measures were generously bestowed. The three men drank in silence, for no toast applicable to the occasion came to mind that would not have sounded flippant.

Watching him narrowly, Faro decided that Kellar was showing remarkable self-control and there was little doubt that he had purged his emotions with the physical act of vomiting.

Kellar nodded in the direction of the fur cloak. 'Where was that found?'

After Superintendent McIntosh had related the details of the discovery, there was a lengthy pause before Kellar said: 'I suppose I must have been the last person to see her, except for the passengers and the madman on the train who murdered her. Fancy choosing my poor silly Mabel as a victim. God knows why . . . '

'Tell me, sir, did you see her on to the train?'

Kellar shook his head. 'No, Inspector. I did not. As a matter of fact, it was snowing and I was already late for my midday lecture. I told her to get a porter, but she insisted that as she had so little luggage with her . . . '

'Did anyone see you return to the house?' asked Faro.

Kellar gave him a mocking look. 'What you mean is, have I an alibi?'

'Something of the sort, sir.' Faro heard McIntosh's shocked intake of breath. 'The maid or the housekeeper – were they in?'

'How the devil do I know whether the servants are in or out? It is one of my strict rules that they keep out of my way entirely, except when they are asked to serve food and so forth. My wife and I value our privacy, that is why we employ the absolute minimum of domestics.'

'Surely the housekeeper—'

'Her most of all. She's only in my house on sufferance – and on twice the salary she's worth – until Mabel gets back . . . '

And Kellar stopped suddenly, his eyes widened, as if this was the first time the full horror of the situation had struck him. 'My God,' he whispered and slumped forward, resting his head in his hands. 'My God – Mabel. She's never coming back – dear God. The poor stupid fool, she's dead, isn't she?'

The Superintendent and Faro exchanged glances and, with McIntosh murmuring platitudes, they withdrew and quietly closed the door behind them.

'Any theories?' asked the Superintendent.

Faro looked at the clock. 'If I hurry, I should just be in time to catch the North Berwick train, with luck the same one that Mrs Kellar travelled on. Since the murder probably took place between Edinburgh and Longniddry, and she would travel in a closed first-class compartment, it's unlikely that the upholstery escaped the murderous onslaught. There must have been blood spattered everywhere.'

'True. And as the evidence of the cloak suggests a struggle, a lot of it also went on to the murderer.'

'We're presuming, of course, that he left the train at Longniddry so perhaps a porter there might have noticed his bloodstained hands or clothes.'

At the door Faro hesitated. 'Might as well check on Dr Kellar's alibi while I'm here.'

'I was just going to suggest that, Faro,' said the Superintendent sternly. 'Find out, if he was late for his lecture that morning, and so forth. Discreet as possible, mind you. Better coming from you than from one of our lads. Think up some sort of excuse to see a timetable, make it sound feasible, will you? Leave you to it. No need to encourage any more gossip than necessary at this stage. There'll be more than enough when his students get wind of this. God help us all.'

Faro watched the Superintendent walk to the other side of the hall with an intense feeling of irritation at having been told how to do his job as if he was just being sent out on his first murder enquiry.

He found the registrar's clerk in his office.

''Morning, Inspector, what can we do for you?'

'We've lost our timetable of Dr Kellar's lectures,' he said casually. It was surprisingly easy. 'Have you a spare copy?'

'Certainly, Sir.'

Faro studied the paper set before him. 'I thought Dr Kellar had a Monday morning lecture.'

The clerk shook his head. 'Not this term, Inspector. Monday is his day off.'

The Superintendent joined him at the door and as they walked towards the Central Office, Faro repeated the clerk's statement.

'Why should Dr Kellar lie about being at his lecture?' said the Superintendent.

'Why indeed, when such matters are so easy to check?'

Things were beginning to look black indeed for the police surgeon, especially as Faro was inclined to disregard Kellar's hint that Mabel's assassin had been a madman on the train. If so, then where was her body?

Logically, it would have been expected to come to light as did the cloak when the snow melted, if it had been pushed out of the train. If not already dead, then appallingly injured and with such considerable loss of blood to be rendered incapable of travelling far. In all probability, she had lain undiscovered, hidden by the snow for the past two weeks.

Faro decided, without a great deal of hope, to examine the railway compartment. A struggle such as the dead woman must have put up would surely have been accompanied by screams for help and even if these had been ignored, it was unlikely that a heavily bloodstained compartment had not yet been reported to the police.

He was brooding on another theory that seriously incriminated Kellar. His wife had never boarded that train. Faro remembered the housekeeper had overheard Kellar shouting that he would take Mrs Kellar 'to the blasted station, or all the way'.

He was now giving serious consideration to the fact that Mrs Kellar had been driven in the brougham through East Lothian and in some lonely spot she had been murdered. Her fur cloak and the knife had then been disposed of on the railway embankment to make it look like a train murder.

As to the whereabouts of her body, no one enjoyed a more advantageous and unique position to commit murder and get away with it than the police surgeon. Dr Kellar was highly skilled at the disposal of corpses by the dissection and distribution of their limbs for anatomical study among his eager medical students.

Chapter Six

Faro soon discovered that there was little hope of asking porters if any of them recalled Mrs Kellar boarding the North Berwick train. He arrived on the platform in time to find that the services of all porters were keenly in demand by anxious passengers emerging from the train, wreathed in heavy clouds of steam.

'All change. All change.'

Seizing the opportunity, Faro sought the guard and introduced himself as investigating a suspected crime in Longniddry.

The guard, Wilson by name, whistled. 'Don't get many crimes in that area. Oh yes, sir, this is my regular train,' he added with a proud and affectionate look at the engine.

'Have I time to have a glance through the first-class carriages?'

'If you can do it quickly, Inspector. We move off again in five minutes.'

'That will be adequate. I wonder if you'd be so good as to accompany me.'

'Why, yes sir. Of course.'

Watching the Inspector's careful examination of the upholstery, Wilson said apologetically, 'The train's fairly new, only two years old, but the upholstery gets dirty quite quickly, as you can see, with all the smoke from the stack and so forth. These carriages are just about ready for a spring clean.'

Far from being pristine, indeed, but as Faro had already deduced, there was nothing resembling widespread blood-stains.

In reply to his question Wilson said, 'Oh yes, sir, we do this same journey back and forward between Edinburgh and Berwick four times each day.'

'Then you would be able to remember if it has been running as usual during the past two weeks.'

'Absolutely, sir.'

'There have been no breakdowns or replacement carriages?'

'Never, sir, without my knowledge. You can rely on that. This is my train,' he said proudly, 'a most reliable engine, never given us a moment's trouble.'

'Could you say definitely whether this train ran as usual at midday on Monday, January 16th?'

The guard grinned. 'It did, sir and I was on it. It was my daughter's first birthday and starting to snow heavily when we left Edinburgh. We were anxious about possible delays. Folks like to get home for their dinners and we have a lot of passengers joining and leaving the train at the intermittent stations.'

'Bearing in mind the snowfall, there were no blockages on the line, even just for a few minutes?'

Wilson thought. 'No, not that day, I'm certain. Everything went smoothly and we arrived in North Berwick on the dot of 12.45.'

'At the time you were checking the tickets, can you remember seeing anyone behaving in what you might consider an odd way?'

'Such as, sir?'

'Well, did you interrupt an argument, for instance?'

Wilson thought for a moment, pushed back his cap and scratched his head. 'No, sir, I can't honestly say that I saw anything at all out of the ordinary. All very normal, the gentlemen hiding behind their newspapers, as always. And the ladies reading or staring out of the window. Very well-behaved travellers, they are. Like their privacy, of course, and that day a lot of them travelled with the blinds drawn.'

'Surely that is unusual in daylight hours?'

'Not at all, sir. The sun is low at this time of year, and what with the glare of the snow, and the smoke, it can be trying on the passengers' eyes.'

'So you don't see much of what's happening inside the compartments.'

'Not a lot. I mind my own business, Inspector,' Wilson added sternly, 'leave them severely alone except when I have to examine the tickets.'

And so creating the perfect opportunity for a murderer, thought Faro hopefully.

'Were the first-class carriages crowded that day?'

Again the guard thought. 'No more than usual.'

'Were any of these compartments empty?'

'There might have been a couple.'

'Can you remember one being occupied by a lady and gentleman travelling together?'

Wilson grinned. 'Oh yes, that was the young honeymooners, bless them. Got on at Musselburgh.'

'Tell me, do you remember a lady travelling that day in a very handsome fur cloak – sable, it was.'

'I wouldn't know sable from water rat, sir,' said Wilson ruefully, 'that's for sure. Besides most of our better-off lady passengers travelling first at this time of year wrap up well in their fur cloaks to keep warm. Was your lady young or old?'

'Middle-aged.'

The guard nodded. 'That's mostly the age that can afford the furs, sir.' He consulted his watch. 'Have to look sharp, sir. Time we were leaving.'

'I think I'll stay on. A ticket to Longniddry, if you please.'

As the train steamed out of Waverley Station, overshadowed by Carlton Hill, Faro considered that the comfort of travelling in a first-class compartment was well worth the extra expense.

He enjoyed rail travel and regretted that it was a fairly

uncommon occurrence in his life. As he studied the passing landscape, reeling down the window to have a good look at the three stations where the train halted before Longniddry, he noted that the journey so far had taken twenty minutes.

Twenty minutes would be more than enough time to stab Mabel Kellar to death with the carving knife in a compartment with the blinds drawn.

But if that was so, then there would have been blood spattered everywhere, far more than could be contained in the fur cloak. The murderer's clothing and hands must also have been stained. Once his gruesome job was completed, he would want to make a speedy exit from the scene of the crime. Having disposed of the evidence he presumably got out himself at Longniddry.

Faro shook his head. The explanation was plausible, he could imagine the scene but one vital question still remained unanswered. What did he do with the body? All he had to do was open the compartment door and push body, cloak and knife out on to the railway line. Otherwise Wilson would have found the body when he was collecting his tickets again after Longniddry and the hue and cry would have been raised immediately.

The snow lay deep on both sides of the line covering the banks. Here and there a shrub or hedgerow was visible, but most of the landscape was hidden under a heavy blanket of snow.

There was another possible explanation for the still missing body. Heavier than the cloak, had it rolled, gathered momentum as it slid down an embankment? Was it still lying entombed in a huge unmelted snowball somewhere along the line?

As they approached Longniddry Station, a biting wind and acrid smoke blew into Faro's face as he leaned out of the window in search of places where a falling body might have lodged. There were none immediately visible and when the platform was in sight he beheld a band of uniformed policemen carefully searching the area surrounding the railway line.

As the train slowed down, they recognised him and shouted, 'Nothing so far, sir. Nothing suspicious. No bloodstained corpse, but we keep hoping.'

Faro lingered, watching the station master collecting tickets. He seemed to know most of the passengers well enough to pass the time of day and greet them by name.

That was hopeful. This was a small station and the people who used it were probably regulars working in Edinburgh or Musselburgh. A stranger, particularly one wearing bloodstained clothes, would surely be remarked upon.

Station Master Andrews was more than willing to chat about this sensational occurrence which had put Longniddry on the map. But Faro was in for a disappointment to his hopes that he might remember a stranger carrying a large brown paper parcel.

'Two weeks, sir.' The man rubbed his forehead. 'That's rather a long time ago. This train's always busy – dinner time and a lot of coming and going between the local stations.'

To Faro's question, he shook his head. 'I think I would have noticed any stranger among the passengers, sir. I have a good memory for faces and it's mostly locals travelling on that train. Always a lot of our ladies with their maids returning from shopping expeditions in Edinburgh.'

He looked at Faro curiously. 'Word certainly does get around fast, Inspector. There was this reporter from the *Scotsman* wanting to know all the details . . . '

Faro groaned. This was the worst possible news. He must try to stop this sensational piece of information being made public, although at the moment there was nothing the press could do to tie it in with the missing Mabel Kellar. As far as everyone but the few Central Office officials knew, Mrs Kellar was still on holiday with her sister at North Berwick.

He just hoped that Ina and Mrs Flynn were not avid newspaper readers.

Trying to sound more casual than he felt, he said, 'He was off his mark very quickly, seeing that the cloak has just been discovered.'

'Yes, Inspector. It was a lucky day for him. He had been down here covering a society wedding in one of the big houses and was waiting for the Edinburgh train when Brown comes rushing down the track carrying the bundle and shouting. "Look at this. I reckon there's been a murder done." Those were his exact words and the reporter was on to it like a shot.'

'Where can I find Brown?'

'There he is now. Over there, crossing the line, just back from his dinner.'

Brown was young and eager. Yes, he found the parcel and took the liberty of unwrapping it, just in case. 'I could see straight away that there'd been foul play.' He paused looking at Faro's expressionless face. 'Been a murder, hasn't there, sir?'

When Faro said cautiously, 'Not necessarily,' Brown continued, 'But it's suspicious, wouldn't you say, sir? All that blood – and a carving knife.'

'But there's no body so far, so there might possibly be some other explanation. And that is what we have to find.'

Brown looked quite dejected.

'Now I'd like you to show me the exact spot where you found the parcel, if you please.'

Leading the way down the line, Brown sounded glum. 'But it is definitely foul play, isn't it, sir? I mean, the woman who wore it must have been stabbed to death, must have lost a lot of blood – and that knife too . . . ' Stopping, he rubbed his foot against the grassy slope. 'It was exactly here, sir. I put this mark against the telegraph pole.'

'Well done,' said Faro, thanking Brown and fending off his eager and curious questions. The lad seemed most reluctant to leave him and, finally watching him wander rather despondently back towards the station building, Faro thought wryly that Brown with his ghoulish relish for crime might have exactly the right brand of enthusiasm they hoped to find in new recruits for the City Police.

He carefully examined the place where the parcel had lain, two hundred yards away from the station on the same side of the line. The station side also gave direct access to the platform for first-class passengers. Close to the ticket barrier, the privileged passengers could leave with a minimum of effort, instead of having to walk along a corridor, the length of a carriage. A fact, decided Faro, imagining the hasty descent and hurried exit from the station, of considerable assistance to Mabel Kellar's murderer.

From where he stood the railway line stretched north and south between the snowy slope of winter fields on one side and on the station entrance side, the Edinburgh road.

Faro lit a pipe thoughtfully and was considering the discovery of the parcel when a uniformed policeman appeared and leaned over the fence.

'Afternoon, Inspector. I've spoken to the farmer over there,' he pointed to the fields. 'But he hasn't seen anyone behaving suspiciously on his property, or carrying a large brown paper parcel. He's a forbidding old man, sir, and I don't think he'd miss much. He also showed me a shotgun he keeps to warn off intruders.'

As Faro wandered back to the platform, he was in time to see Station Master Andrews chasing and capturing a youth of about fourteen. Holding him firmly by the coat collar, Andrews demanded, 'Travelling without paying your fare, eh? Is that your little game?'

Grumbling, red-faced, the youth took out a coin and handed it over.

'All right, I'll accept it this time. But try that again and we'll get the police to you.'

Andrews grinned at Faro. 'There's always one of these townies tries it. Manage to hide from the guard on the way down and then they jump off the train, lurking about in the waiting-room or the lavatory until they think they can slip through the barrier without paying.' A bell sounded shrilly inside. 'That's the Edinburgh train from Newcastle approaching now, sir. You'll have to get across the bridge, sharp as you can.'

As he settled back comfortably in the compartment and was carried to Edinburgh, Faro thought about the youth who had hidden in the waiting-room. If he'd managed to evade Station Master Andrew's sharp eyes, then what was to stop Mabel Kellar's murderer also washing the blood off his hands in the lavatory and then calmly crossing the bridge and boarding the Newcastle train back to Edinburgh as he had done?

When they reached Waverley, Faro made a mental note to have his constables carry out a routine check at the station. Meanwhile, on the off-chance that a porter might have remembered putting Mrs Kellar on the train or that the ticket collector, like Andrews, had a good memory for faces, he lingered at the barrier.

When the last passenger had departed, he described Mrs Kellar and asked, 'Do you recall any lady like that boarding the 12 o'clock North Berwick train?'

'A couple of weeks ago, sir? Now that's a poser. Fur cloak, you say, middle-aged? That's what most of the first-class ladies wear in this weather.'

As Faro was walking away, a porter who had been listening curiously and intently to this conversation came forward.

'Excuse me, sir, couldn't help overhearing. You say two weeks ago? Well, I remember there was a middle-aged lady, in a very fine fur cloak. She called for a porter at the station entrance, asked for the North Berwick train. She was very upset, poor soul, in tears.'

'Did she get out of a carriage?'

'Oh yes, sir, a brougham.'

If Mabel Kellar had travelled on the train alone then this information threw a completely new light on to the evidence and they were seeking a faceless murderer.

'The man who was driving the brougham? Can you remember what he was like?'

The porter shook his head. 'Not really, sir. But he was in a terrible temper. Shouting at her.'

'Shouting – like what? Do you remember?'

'Oh yes. Abuse, that's what. "Go to him and damn you both. Damn you both to hell."' The porter paused. 'I suppose that was her husband and she was going off with another man and taking the laddie with her.'

'Laddie? What laddie?'

'There was a wee chap with her, clinging to her hand. About nine or ten. And he was fair upset too.'

Thanking the porter, Faro walked away. So much for grand theories, advanced and demolished within minutes, he thought, making his way back to the Central Office.

Chapter Seven

Calling in at Sheridan Place to collect some papers from his study, Faro was delighted to find Vince had returned late that morning. Already well-cosseted and pampered by Mrs Brook, he looked up with a grin from reading the newspaper and greeted his stepfather.

'I have to rush out again, lad, but did you have a good holiday?'

'Superb. I'll tell you all about it at dinner. Bought a *Times* to read on the train. Have you seen this?'

A small paragraph read: 'Mysterious Discovery on Railway Line near Longniddry. The discovery of a woman's bloodstained fur cloak and a carving knife has led to an immediate investigation by Edinburgh City Police into the possibility of foul play.'

When Faro groaned, Vince said, 'Fame at last, eh? Is this one of your cases? Has all this happened since I've been away?'

'I'm just back from Longniddry.'

'Really? Tell me more.'

'Vince, lad,' Faro sat down heavily in the chair opposite and took his stepson's hands. 'I have to prepare you for a shock. We have reason to believe that the cloak belonged to Mabel Kellar.'

Vince laughed. 'How extraordinary. Then what on earth was it doing on the railway line. Stolen, was it?'

'We don't know. Vince, I warned you the news was bad. Mrs Kellar has been missing since the morning you went on holiday.'

'But she only went to her sister's at North Berwick.'
'She never got there.'
'But—'
'Vince. We think she's been murdered.'
'Murdered? Mabel? Oh dear God – no.'
And Faro was later to find some significance in the fact that Vince's cry of agony was considerably more heartfelt than Dr Kellar's reaction to the grim discovery that pointed to his wife's brutal murder.
'I have to go now, but I'll be back shortly.' He put his hand on Vince's shoulder. 'We'll talk about it then.'
Vince declined supper that evening. 'Mrs Brook fed me more than enough when I arrived home. I couldn't eat another bite, especially now – with all this about Mabel. Come on, Stepfather, tell me.'
As carefully as he could and without displaying any more emotion than he would have shown had the missing woman been unknown to either of them, Faro went carefully over the details, from Kellar informing Superintendent McIntosh that Mabel was missing to his own visit to Longniddry Station and the subsequent revelations.
Vince was silent, trying to take in all these crucial facts and at the same time trying not to link them with that dear woman who had befriended him. At last he spoke, wearily, as if the effort of remembering was too much for him.
'Did you know I called on her that – that very morning on my way to the station?'
'The housekeeper told me. Oh, I'm sorry, lad.'
'Don't be sorry for me, Stepfather. Be sorry for her murderer,' he said harshly. 'Because if the law doesn't get him and hang him, then I'll take the matter of justice into my own hands.'
Appalled at such a prospect, Faro said, 'I don't think that'll be necessary.'
'You know who did it then?'
'We have a good idea.'

'And you haven't arrested him yet? For God's sake, Stepfather, he might escape.'

'Be calm, lad, be calm. As you were almost the last person to see Mabel, anything you can tell us about that visit would be of enormous help.'

Vince stared out of the window at the snow-clad slope of Arthur's Seat. When at last he spoke, his voice was overcome with emotion. 'Thinking about it, I realise that she was trying to conceal how desperately upset she was that morning. There'd been that unholy row with Kellar after we left. Just one more but this time serious enough for her to be seeking refuge with her sister. Actually leaving her husband, as he rightly deserves. She should have done so long ago . . . '

'What was this row about? Did she tell you.'

'She spared me the exact details, hinted at a very unpleasant post-mortem on the culinary disasters of the dinner-party and that Kellar hadn't spared her. Anyway, I offered to escort her to the railway station as I was catching a train there myself. She refused. Said she wasn't ready to leave. Packing to complete, instructions for the housekeeper and so forth, very nervous and upset.'

Vince's words took on a sinister meaning. That had been his own impression of Mrs Kellar during the dinner. Of course, it might not indicate more than a nervous disposition heightened and upset by the new housekeeper's delay in preparing and serving the courses.

Faro rubbed his chin thoughtfully, as he remembered how the guests had stirred uncomfortably in their chairs, reluctant witnesses to their host's anger. That scene at least had survived the boredom of the evening.

'It would have made more sense if she'd taken the carving knife to him. There were moments when I felt like it, I can tell you,' said Vince.

'I distinctly remember you saying so, lad,' said Faro drily. 'It's a good job we're not dealing with a missing Dr Kellar or you might well be the chief suspect.'

Vince shrugged as if getting rid of Kellar might have been worth it. 'You remember, Stepfather, how frightful it all was.'

Faro nodded. 'If only we had paid more attention to the subtle undercurrents, for undercurrents there should have been that night. Some hint of the monstrous events to come, some plan in the mind of the murderer.'

'You mean the murderer was with us that evening? Surely not?'

'It has been my experience that when a murder is committed, one need look no further than the family circle to find the guilty party.'

'Not in this case,' said Vince firmly. 'And if you're hinting at Kellar himself, I think you're miles out. Never Kellar. Think again, Stepfather and you'll see I'm right. With so much to lose. I assure you his pride is far greater than his passion and he would never do anything to prejudice that knighthood in the offing.

'No,' – again Vince shook his head emphatically – 'you must be wrong this time, Stepfather. Kellar is much too emotionless to go for his wife with the carving knife. You have to love deeply to hate deeply and, quite frankly, I'd be prepared to bet that he hardly notices that Mabel exists. As for loving her, well, I imagine that part of their life was very brief and very long ago.'

He shuddered. 'I feel it is much more likely that she succumbed to the frenzy of some madman who boarded the train, found her alone and – and—' his voice broke into a sob.

'I know, lad. I know.' Faro patted his arm sympathetically. 'That is the answer one always hopes to find, the stranger on whom the bereaved family can vent their own grief and anger. Rarely, alas, is this the case. Besides,' he added in tones of consolation that he was far from feeling, 'the cloak and knife might appear to be damning evidence, but until the body is recovered we have no definite proof that murder had been committed.'

Even as he said the words, Faro had reached his own grim conclusions. If Kellar was indeed her murderer, then Mabel would never be found. Faro was not in the least doubt of that, with a horrific certainty of how her body had been disposed of. He must spare Vince from that knowledge as long as he could.

'The motive could have been robbery, Stepfather. She had a lot of very valuable jewellery. Inherited. Not from Kellar. He was too mean to spend money on frivolities. She was locking up her jewel case while I talked to her.'

'Can you describe it?'

'Yes. Red leather, with brass fastenings.'

And she hadn't taken it with her. Faro remembered it lying on the dressing table along with the silver brushes and toilette set.

'That's it, Stepfather. I've just remembered something. "People to see."'

'People to see?'

'Yes. Those were her exact words. "I have instructions to give to Mrs Flynn and people to see before I go." I wonder who they were.'

Faro sighed. 'Have you any theories about how her cloak came to be found on the railway line then?'

Vince formed the picture in his mind and closed his eyes against it. 'You say Kellar identified it as Mabel's. Surely if he were guilty . . . '

'Guilty or innocent, lad, what else could he have done? Since the housekeeper and the maid would no doubt also recognise the cloak, all he would have done was to have proved himself a liar. He even read the label inside and told us that was indeed Mrs Kellar's furrier and that it would be easy enough to check.'

'That doesn't sound like a guilty man to me,' said Vince.

'Unless he's also a very clever one,' Faro replied drily.

'Kellar is a beast but I still can't believe it was him,' Vince protested obstinately. 'Now if you were to suspect the Mad Bart . . . '

'Unfortunately we can't fix murders to suit our own prejudices,' said Faro sternly. 'I too hope you're right about Kellar being innocent for quite a different reason. Can you imagine the furore of public reaction when they learn that the Edinburgh City Police have a surgeon in their midst who has murdered his wife? McIntosh is afraid that, used by the wrong people,this could be the stepping stone for riot, for the breakdown of law and order. A bit drastic, but I see his point.'

'God help Kellar, guilty or innocent, Stepfather. Once the story gets abroad his reputation will be finished. You know how such muck clings to a man. I can't see him surviving such a scandal, either.'

'At this stage, all I am doing is piecing together, with some difficulty, the few facts we have to go on. Long experience has taught me to suspect anyone and everyone however remotely connected. And always to be ready for the unexpected.'

Faro paused before adding, 'It's no use you trying to be fair-minded and putting in a good word for him. I'm perfectly aware that you didn't care for him at all. And he's not popular with his students, either.'

He put a hand on Vince's shoulder. 'The first step in putting together the story of her last hours lies within the Kellar house and you, I'm afraid, are witness to that last hour. Her state of mind and so forth could be valuable evidence. We'll need a statement from you, of course.' Seeing Vince's still, stricken face, he added, 'I wish it was otherwise, lad, and that we could avoid having you dragged into this sorry business.'

'Don't worry about me, Stepfather. I'll be glad to say anything that will put a rope around her murderer's vile neck.'

Vince went to the sideboard and poured himself a whisky. After a moment he said, 'All I know is what I've told you. That she seemed extremely agitated and upset by the row with Kellar.'

'Yes, I know. But I keep going further back than that. To the beginning of it all. The dinner party.'

'The last straw, do you think?'

'I'm considering her distress that night. Are we being too hasty blaming it all on the burnt roast. Was there another cause? Could she have been afraid?'

'Of course she was afraid, Stepfather. Of her husband's brutal ill-humour.'

Faro shook his head. 'A storm in a teacup, lad. Hardly an uncommon occurrence, even in the most civilised of families. Situations regarding ruined food and the feeling that the wife is totally to blame for the servants' shortcomings. Happens all the time, lad. The only difference was that Kellar didn't bother to restrain his wrath until the guests were gone.'

'They quarrelled, Stepfather. In front of all of us.'

'Not they – he quarrelled. The high words all came from Kellar. His wife uttered a few tearful protests. No, lad, quarrel is definitely a misnomer. Besides, all married couples bicker over domestic details.'

Vince regarded him steadily. 'Do they indeed? Then that makes me all the more eager to embrace permanent bachelordom.'

Faro laughed. 'If you do, then you will be throwing away an extremely valuable parcel unopened simply because the wrapping is slightly torn. You will never know the good things inside.'

'From what Mabel Kellar told me . . . ' Vince began darkly.

'My dear lad, I beg you not to read too much into the revelations of an aggrieved wife. They do tend to exaggerate.'

How to tactfully point out to his young stepson his invidious position – that women, especially childless women of a certain age and social standing, were too often bored with a busy husband's neglect and discreetly sought male attention elsewhere. And what better opportunity for a gentle romance than a husband's handsome young assistant brought into their orbit? He looked at his stepson with compassion. This young and vulnerable lad still walking the cloudy dreams of chivalry, more than ready to be flattered by an older woman's interest, eager to lend a sympathetic ear and – perhaps a little too obviously – wear his heart on his sleeve.

Vince looked uncomfortable and growled. 'You know me too well, don't you.'

'Almost as well as I know married couples.' Faro laughed. 'An unholy row which sounds like pistols at fifteen paces to the embarrassed onlookers would be dismissed by the couple themselves as a harmless tiff, an almost everyday event which ends in a tearful reconciliation on the wife's part, with both firmly believing they have the victory. Such matters as a housekeeper's incompetence, lad, don't usually lead to murder.'

'If the shoe had been on the other foot, however . . . '

'Mrs Kellar didn't strike me as a woman of such pride that she would want to commit murder because she had been made to look an idiot before their guests.'

'You forget one thing, Stepfather. She adores – adored him.' Vince closed his eyes tightly as if to shut off the realisation that he would never see her again. 'Incredible as it may seem and despite his abominable treatment, she would always go back for more. God alone knows why. And she would never look at another man.' Vince sighed heavily and added dramatically. 'I would have taken her away, you know, Stepfather. Protected her, worshipped her.'

'Then you would have been the world's greatest idiot,' said Faro furiously, thumping the table. 'Marriage with a woman more than twice your age.'

'I wasn't talking of marriage,' said Vince softly. 'Besides, age doesn't matter.'

'Not at twenty and forty, but what about in ten years', twenty years' time. When you are my age, and she is sixty. A mistress of sixty.' Faro laughed harshly. 'Chivalry is all very well. Be a knight in shining armour in theory but, I beg you, don't make me angry by talking absolute nonsense, lad.'

There was a moment's silence then Vince said contemptuously, 'Kellar is just the kind of man to marry for money, knowing she was the Mad Bart's heiress.'

'So that was the reason.'

'I know exactly what you're thinking,' was the defensive reply. 'Mabel isn't in the least pretty. But once you get to know her, you forget all about looks. She has such a divine nature, such a delicious sense of humour. So wise and warm-hearted. So different to all those silly giggling dolls, the simpering misses whom it's been my misfortune to meet up to now. If you'd ever known her, Stepfather, you'd know what I mean. No man could have resisted her.'

No man being Vince himself, thought Faro. Sadly one couldn't tell the lad that, given time, simpering misses of eighteen also learn wisdom – at least most do by the time they are forty – and that the wisdom and warm-heartedness and a sense of humour which he found so irresistible are time's compensation for growing older.

'Anyway,' continued Vince, 'a person's looks, like their age, mean nothing really. Not once you get to know them.'

Faro's eyebrows shot upwards in surprise. Here was a change indeed. How deadly accurate had been Cupid's arrows on this unfortunate lad who had been willing to lose his heart ever since boyhood to every pretty face.

'Surely you've noticed, Stepfather, how often handsome men choose quite plain wives. Like the peacock in all his radiant glory – and look at the poor peahen, without a fine feather to her name.'

'Nature has been most unfair in that respect.'

'Of course she has – but deuced clever too. Reason being that Nature's only reason for distribution of fine feathers – on all species – was intended for marvels of reproduction.

It was necessary to attract females in droves, the more the merrier, for a species to survive and multiply. After all, Nature never planned that males should take only one mate, that was man's mistake when he became civilised.'

Faro laughed. 'You do have some far-fetched theories, lad. And grand as all this is for your peahens, civilised humans behaving like barnyard fowls would have caused even more trouble in the world than we are in at present. And that was why the good Lord ordained that what was good for the animals going into the ark two by two was also good for his best creation, man.'

'Kellar didn't abide by that rule. He liked the ladies.'

'I rather suspected he might.'

The doorbell pealed.

'Expecting anyone?' asked Faro.

'Oh, I forgot. Rob said he would come round, to hear all about Walter and the Austrian visit. I could put him off. I don't really feel up to going out tonight.'

'You go. Do you good. Besides, I have a report to write. We'll talk about it when you get back.'

Chapter Eight

Faro did not see Vince again that evening. Finding his friend in very low spirits, Rob had suggested that there were places where sorrows might be effectively drowned in some of the more exciting howffs down Leith Walk.

Meanwhile Faro gathered together all his information on the case of Mabel Kellar, missing and now presumed murdered by person or persons unknown. That, he decided even as he began his preliminary report, wasn't quite true. Apart from the theory of the madman on the train, he was certain that her murderer would be found much nearer home.

Next morning, Vince came into the dining-room looking extremely weary and heavy-eyed, as if he had slept little. Seeing Faro about to depart for the Central Office Vince summoned a wan smile. 'If you can spare a minute, Stepfather, stay and talk to me while I have breakfast.' He pointed to the papers Faro was gathering together. 'I presume these relate to Mabel.'

Faro nodded. 'Just my findings so far. Possible suspects, motives and so forth.'

Vince held out his hand. 'May I?'

'Are you sure?'

'Yes, Stepfather. I've always tried to help in the past and this time, more than any other, I have a personal score to settle.'

'All right, lad. Read it if you like. It won't take long.'

Vince scanned the two pages. 'I think you can dismiss

the maid and housekeeper as possible suspects. Both are relative newcomers to the Kellar household and they have nothing but praise for Mabel. Besides they have no motive.'

He paused and shook his head. 'It would have made a lot more sense if Kellar had been the victim. I can just imagine him presenting an irresistible murder target for an ill-used domestic.'

'Does anything strike you as significant about this case, Vince?'

Vince thought for a moment. 'Yes. This is a man's crime. All the evidence points to a strong man, wielding the carving knife and,' he added with a grimace, 'disposing of the body. You agree?'

'My conclusions entirely.'

'So it would seem that the doctor is the prime suspect.'

'As yet, yes.'

Vince frowned. 'There is a possibility, of course, that there was no motive. That one of his fits of irritation with Mabel became uncontrollable, carried him across the threshold of normality and he suffered a brainstorm.'

'Aren't you forgetting the carving knife?'

'Yes, I am. Of course one hardly embarks on a peaceful journey to the railway station carrying a carving knife. I agree that has very sinister implications.'

'But if it had all been carefully planned – let us suppose that we are right and Kellar tricked his wife into believing he was driving her to North Berwick and then murdered her. Surely he disposed of that damning evidence in a remarkably clumsy fashion?'

'I agree, Stepfather, but again this is not beyond the bounds of possibility. In a medical study of the behaviour of wife-murderers, even the most fiendish and calculating have been known to give way to moments of blind panic.'

Faro tried to picture the scene: Kellar poised over his wife's dead body, in that terrible moment when the red murder light faded from his eyes. Horrified, sated with blood lust, had he seen the railway line as a hell-sent opportunity of diverting suspicion?

He glanced at his notes. 'The only other male employees, I gather, are a jobbing gardener.'

'I've met him. Had a word about roses – his passion. He's a harmless old lad who comes in twice a week in the summer and is never allowed to set foot inside the house. Not much for him to do this time of year.'

'There's also an occasional coachman.'

'He would be from a hiring firm Kellar and all the doctors use. Ambley's at Newington Road.'

'I'll have the constables make a routine check.'

'I doubt whether that'll reveal any motives for Mabel's murder.'

'Fragments, lad. That's what we're after. Minute pieces of information, observation. They are most often the pieces of the puzzle which seem quite irrelevant but when put together give us the face – and the motive – of our murderer.'

'I hardly think you need bother with exhaustive enquiries in this case. If Kellar did it, we only need to know why, where and how he disposed of – of her,' said Vince.

'Know anything about her sister, Mrs Findlay-Cupar? I shall have to go and see her in North Berwick.'

'I gather that they were very close, quite devoted. Mabel talked a lot about Tiz, that's her nickname. I think she could be ruled out of your list of suspects. What about her uncle? He's mad enough to do anything.'

Faro shook his head. 'I think we know that the Mad Bart's reputation is based on eccentricity, rather than dementia.'

'Well, as she's his heiress,' said Vince dubiously, 'I'd say he would bear some investigation.'

Faro smiled at his grim expression. 'Prejudice, lad. Prejudice.'

'Of course it isn't,' replied Vince crossly.

'All right. Item one, his hands are twisted with

rheumatism. As a doctor you must have noticed he has difficulty lighting a pipe so I don't imagine he'd be very deft with a carving knife. Item two, if Mabel was killed on the train, then we're looking for an agile man, strong, quick-witted, quick-moving. I think we can safely dismiss from our list of suspects an infirm old chap, who shambles along with the aid of a stick.'

'I suppose strong, quick-witted and quick-moving couldn't possibly include Mrs Eveline Shaw either,' said Vince. 'I see you put a tick against her name.'

'Not as a suspect. Only because as Mrs Kellar's dearest friend and companion – isn't that how she described her to us? – she might know something important.'

'In what way?'

'In the way of confidences. Something from the past that would shed an interesting light on an apparently blameless life.'

'I can assure you . . . '

But Vince's assurances went unuttered. The doorbell announced the arrival of yet another of his young doctor friends, who was calling for news about Walter.

Faro left the house very thoughtfully. His discussion with Vince had revealed only one true suspect. And that was, as it had always been, Kellar. Most damning of all was the absence of a body and although all the evidence so far silently accused Mabel's husband, as yet no motive for her murder was apparent.

He was not looking forward to confronting Kellar with his false alibi and demanding from him a satisfactory account of his movements that Monday, when he was not giving a lecture, as he had led them to believe. Here was another inconsistency in behaviour. Why had he told such a stupid lie when he must have known that it could be checked?

Even more important, Faro was aware of a nagging feeling of unease, insistent as a dull toothache, at the back of his mind. He knew what that meant. He had overlooked something vital, some very significant detail had not registered on that first visit to the house.

He decided that a vague excuse for another look around the house would be worthwhile, again choosing a time when, hopefully, the master was absent.

Considering that physical exercise was always beneficial in the process of mind-clearing, he walked the short distance to the Grange, having to take frequent refuge from the spray of unpleasantly brown slush sent flying by the wheels of passing coaches. He found that his concentration was needed less in agitating his powers of deduction than in keeping his feet as his boots slipped constantly on the treacherous expanses of frozen snow. He was glad indeed to reach the drive leading to the Kellar house although walking was still hazardous. At last he reached the front door and with his hand on the bell, he heard his name.

The maid Ina was approaching from the direction of the coach-house, slithering across the icy surface, hampered by a pail and scrubbing brush.

'Sorry to keep you waiting, Inspector,' she said breathlessly. 'I've been cleaning the master's carriage. Such a mess it's always in. He goes shooting on a Wednesday afternoon and then he complains to us that the upholstery was all stained.'

Faro was hardly listening. A bloodstained carriage. Was this what he had been expecting to find, that vital missing clue?

As if she had read his mind, Ina gave him a sideways glance and with a small shudder, whispered, 'I couldn't get it clean so when I showed it to Mrs Flynn, she said it looked like blood to her. I came over all queasy. But Mrs Flynn says what can we expect with the kind of work the master does.'

'Shooting game can make quite a mess,' said Faro in reassuring tones, so as not to alarm her.

She shook her head. 'He doesn't put them inside the brougham. Mrs Kellar would never allow that. Smelly stuff. Has a special box for his rabbits and birds at the back.'

Faro decided not to panic her by asking to inspect the carriage. He resolved to make a discreet and solitary visit to the coach-house a little later, after learning more about the stained upholstery from Mrs Flynn.

Leaving Ina in the hall, he found the housekeeper in her gloomy retreat below stairs. Almost dark, it was one of those winter days that is never really light and the hours designated daytime slide imperceptibly into night at about three in the afternoon. In the dim light from the high barred windows, Mrs Flynn was rolling pastry on the kitchen table. She stared at him over her spectacles and resumed her task without comment.

'Ina let me in. I met her coming from the coach-house. Seems she's been having problems cleaning the brougham.'

As he spoke to her, he wondered how on earth anyone managed to prepare food with little more than a feeble gas jet and the firelight from an indifferent blaze. Presumably domestic servants who live subterranean existences in large houses are like cats and of necessity have to develop their faculties for hunting in the dark.

'Oh yes, the master likes it cleaned every time he uses it, at least twice a week according to him, but being on notice, I forgot and I wasn't reminded by the mistress before she left.' Her cold, he noticed was worse, and her voice fainter than ever. 'I've had a lot to do, so it got left. The master complained the other day. Just like a man, never notice anything but what's wrong. Suddenly he was shouting about how dirty it was. I sent Ina out but she couldn't get it clean. The upholstery was badly marked.'

'Have you any idea what caused the marks?'

She shrugged. 'Couldn't really say, Inspector. I said to Ina when it wouldn't come out that it might be blood. She said she'd faint. But I said with his work, what can you expect? I told her salt's the thing that moves blood, works every time.'

So that piece of evidence which could have been damning might also have disappeared.

'Is there anything else I can do for you, sir?'

'I would like to have another look at Mrs Kellar's bedroom.'

She nodded. 'I'm sure that will be all right, Inspector. You know the way. I'll come up directly.'

He was glad of the chance to look around alone, but that quick inspection told him nothing. Everything was pristine, neat, as it had been the first time. He had a quick look in the wardrobe and the drawers opened without noise. He closed them almost hastily, with an apologetic feeling of guilt at the idea of examining all those elegant, lace-bedecked items of intimate feminine attire.

If Mrs Kellar was unhappy then it wasn't from the lack of worldly possessions and he thought of his dear Lizzie with sudden compassion. In all their married life she never possessed more than 'one for best, two for everyday'. The sad thing was that she felt that three of everything was a matter for pride, not deprivation.

Again he touched the silver brushes, toilette set and locked jewel case. Faro lifted it and it felt heavy. Perhaps that was the reason she had left it behind.

He stared at his own reflection in the mirror and saw Mrs Flynn watching him, her stout shape framed by the door.

'Everything all right, sir?'

'Seems to be.' He felt the statement needed further qualification and added, 'Always have to have a second look, you know.'

Waiting for him to leave, she closed the door and followed him downstairs. As Faro picked up his hat, she took from the hall table a newspaper, and opened it so as not to disturb the folds. 'I often have a quick glance, before the master sees it. I wonder if you can tell me what this is all about?'

She handed the folded paper to him and he read:

Gruesome Discovery on Railway Line

A railway worker Ian Brown of Longniddry today discovered a large parcel containing a woman's sable cloak of considerable value and a carving knife, lying by the side of the line at Longniddry Station. Both items which had lain under the snow for several days were heavily stained with blood and Edinburgh City Police have been called in to investigate this discovery.

Faro returned it to her and she said anxiously, 'The mistress was wearing her sable cloak, as you know, when she went to North Berwick. Has this anything to do with her disappearance?'

'We're looking into it, Mrs Flynn, that is all I can tell you at the moment.'

'Ina will have told you that one of the carving knives has gone.'

'Yes, she did.' Faro hoped his reply was unconcerned.

'Oh, well, I suppose that's all right then.'

She sounded relieved and Faro smiled. 'Carving knives aren't exactly unique, Mrs Flynn.'

He didn't want to scare the woman or Ina or let them get the impression that they were living in a house where the master had done in the mistress and, knowing his terrible temper, they might be next on the list.

Making sure that he was unobserved, Faro made a detour to the coach-house. The door was unlocked and the brougham was sparkling clean, the air redolent with the smell of cleaning fluid. He inspected the upholstery with its barely visible stains. There was no way of identifying the faint yellow marks now or testing out the new experiments Vince had told him about, of distinguishing human and animal blood.

Faro hailed a passing cab near the Grange. Unless Dr Kellar could produce a convincing alibi, things looked black indeed for him and as Faro was set down outside

Surgeons Hall, he had a feeling they weren't going to get any brighter for a very long time.

He did not relish the forthcoming interview. Kellar had deliberately misled them regarding his presence at a lecture on the morning his wife disappeared. If that was a sign of guilt, then he must be in a greater panic than they had realised.

There was also the matter of the bloodstained carriage. If this had been the result of Kellar's grisly murder of his wife, most likely on the way to North Berwick, then he was behaving in a remarkably naive fashion by drawing attention to it.

From his own experience with police procedure, Kellar must be perfectly aware that in a murder case, the victim's spouse is always the first, and most likely, suspect. Faro could only make the excuse of Kellar's notorious vanity, his assumption that his own connection with the Edinburgh City Police, a knighthood in the offing, rendered him beyond suspicion.

Chapter Nine

Faro's arrival coincided with Kellar emerging from the dissecting room, whose odours heavily disguised with antiseptic still clung to him, an unpleasant miasma. He did not look overjoyed at Faro's presence and walked briskly down the corridor. Without lessening his pace, he looked over his shoulder, demanded brusquely, 'Well, and what do you want?'

Faro groaned inwardly. This was hardly a promising start. 'Only a few facts to check, sir.' He tried in vain to sound nonchalant. 'If you will be so good as to spare me the time.'

'Very well,' said Kellar. 'Follow me. You know the way.' Ushered into the miserable room that served as office, Faro was not invited to be seated, an indication, he gathered, that this interview was unwelcome and was not to be prolonged a moment longer than necessary.

'What is it now, Inspector?' Kellar asked impatiently. 'As you can see, I'm a busy man.'

'I went to your house earlier today hoping to see you there.'

Kellar smiled grimly, seeing through this flimsy excuse. 'I am always at Surgeons Hall during the working week at this hour. You should know that, Inspector.'

'But not on Mondays apparently,' Faro reminded him.

'Mondays?' As if a new thought struck him, Kellar said, 'Mondays – no, as a matter of fact, I'm not.'

'So you weren't lecturing at all on the day you took your wife to the station to catch the North Berwick train.'

Kellar gave an impatient shrug. 'No. Obviously I wasn't.'

'Then why, sir, did you indicate—'

Kellar interrupted with an impatient gesture. 'Indicate? I indicated nothing. It was mere aberration, that's all. I forgot completely what day of the week it was.'

Faro tried not to look as disbelieving as he felt. Strange that a husband should forget the day of the week that his wife disappeared. One would imagine such information would be indelibly fixed.

'You let your wife believe that you were going to be late for a lecture.'

Kellar's head jerked up sharply. 'How do you know what I let my wife believe, Faro?'

'You were overheard outside your front door.'

'Overheard? By domestics, I suppose.' Kellar raised his eyes heavenward in a despairing gesture. 'Wasting time spying on their betters when they should be going about their business, which is what we pay them for. This is outrageous, Inspector.'

Faro ignored Kellar's growing anger. 'Perhaps you could remember where you spent the afternoon of Monday, 16th January. That would be of considerable help.'

'Help? Help, in what way?' Kellar sounded surprised and then seeing Faro's sternly guarded expression, he laughed softly. 'Oh, I see. I see. So what do you want me to tell you?'

'Anything that would account for your movements, sir.'

'An alibi, is that it?' Kellar sounded faintly amused.

'Yes, sir, as you know that is quite usual.'

'Usual, in what way usual?'

Kellar wasn't going to make it easy, thought Faro. Every move would have to be laboriously spelled out.

'Just so that you can be cleared—'

Kellar's eyebrows shot upwards. 'Cleared? Do I take it from that remark, you are hinting that I – I am under suspicion, that you seriously believe I had something to do with my wife's disappearance.'

When Faro could think of no suitable reply that evaded the truth, Kellar shouted, 'My God, man, how dare you make such a vile assumption. This is preposterous, do you hear? Preposterous.'

'So is murder, sir.' And in an effort to calm him, Faro added quickly, 'As a police surgeon you know that such enquiries are routine and that everyone connected with a murder victim, especially his or her own household, is under suspicion.'

'Aren't you presuming rather a lot, Inspector?'

'We'll only know that, sir, when we find your wife's murderer.'

'Or her body.'

Faro thought he detected a gleam of satisfaction in Kellar's eyes as he added, 'Don't let us forget the absence of that vital ingredient, the *corpus delicti*.'

'I don't think anyone, not even you, sir, could dispute the fact that the evidence up to now looks uncommonly like foul play.'

Kellar sobered at once. 'I see,' he said slowly and, thrusting out his upper lip, he gazed steadily at the ceiling as if words of inspiration might suddenly appear across its grimy expanse. 'I mostly spend Mondays doing work of my own, in my study. So I expect that is how I was occupied when I returned from the railway station.'

'Presumably Mrs Flynn or the housemaid would be able to confirm this, sir.'

'Of course they would not,' said Kellar irritably. 'It is my policy to assiduously avoid contact with domestics at all times.'

His tone of distaste made it sound like avoidance of lepers. 'When I go to my study and I am working on a paper or lecture notes, I am not to be disturbed. My instructions are very strict on that point. I may only be approached in direst necessity.'

'What about meal times, sir?'

Kellar stared at him as if the suggestion was mad or

highly improper. 'I communicate with domestics by leaving notes on the hall table.'

'Did you do so that day?'

Kellar looked at him narrowly. 'You know, Inspector, I really can't remember.' He paused and then added triumphantly. 'Oh yes, I can. Now it comes back to me. I didn't return home. I had an errand to do for my wife. Of course, of course.'

That was safe enough, thought Faro grimly. And difficult to confirm or deny in the prevailing circumstances. 'What kind of an errand would that be?' he asked.

'I was to take some garments across to her friend Mrs Shaw in Regent Crescent. The housekeeper had been given instructions to clear out the attic and while so doing had come across some infant garments.' He paused and added hurriedly, 'From the early years of our marriage when we had, er, anticipations. Mabel is very well disposed towards Mrs Shaw, and wished her to have these for her wee boy.'

A longer pause followed while Kellar smiled at Faro, as if inviting comment on such generosity. Then in his sudden burst of laughter, Faro thought he detected relief.

'Of course I had forgotten because it was all so unimportant. I had dismissed it from my mind entirely. After I set Mrs Kellar down at the station, I drove directly to Mrs Shaw's home. As a token of her gratitude, she was kind enough to offer me luncheon.'

Frowning, he thought for a moment. 'I found her greatly in need of fresh air, to cheer her spirits. So I took her and little Barnaby for a drive, well wrapped up, of course. We had to cut it short when the snow began to fall rather heavily again. I dined at the Surgeons' Club that evening. You can easily confirm this, if you wish.'

He looked across at Faro. 'Well, Inspector, are you satisfied?'

'It helps considerably, Dr Kellar.'

'No doubt you will wish to speak to Mrs Shaw. I am

sure she will remember the afternoon we spent together.'

Faro thanked him and left, resolving to interview Mrs Shaw immediately, before Kellar had a chance to communicate with her, on the unlikely chance that the two were in collusion.

He made his way on foot as swiftly as possible down the High Street, his progress impeded by the maze of luckenbooths. He had forgotten that this was market day. The din of stall-keepers yelling their wares, combined with smells of fish and vegetables and many less agreeable human odours made concentration impossible.

Walking in the direction of Regent Crescent, head down against the icy blast from the Firth of Forth, Faro saw the Palace and Abbey of Holyroodhouse stripped of all romance. Inadequately sheltered by skeletal trees whose feeble thin branches moaned back and forth in a pathetic protest against the sleet-like rain, the scene was one of direst misery, a monument of inescapable mourning for a Scotland lost for ever with the passing of the Stuarts.

With Mrs Shaw's house in view, Faro mentally rehearsed the forthcoming interview, bearing in mind the new turn of events. If Kellar had gone directly to Mrs Shaw's and spent most of the afternoon with her, then he could not possibly have murdered his wife.

And if not Kellar, then who? With an alibi for the main suspect, this would cease to be an open and shut case. The net must be opened wide to admit the usual exhaustive routine enquiries, for identity and possible motives of murderer or murderers, as well as her missing body. A bleak prospect indeed, Faro suspected, with a trail already cold as the snow which had so conveniently hidden the first evidence of possible murder.

Regent Crescent overlooked the grounds of Holyrood Palace and he soon identified the handsome Georgian house in which Mrs Eveline Shaw lived, by the grand piano in the window. Faro thought himself fortunate to have found her at home or, more correctly, encamped around a rather small fire. They made a pretty picture playing on the rug together, the lovely fair-haired young mother, the sturdy baby with his expressive velvet brown eyes, but they needed a gentler, less forbidding setting. Piano apart, the large drawing-room with its lofty ceiling could have accommodated a whole floor of Sheridan Place. Sparsely furnished, it suggested that the tenant had newly taken up residence.

There was none of the solid furniture, the family portraits, the photographs draped with mourning that he would have expected to find in the home of an affluent young widow whose officer husband had died recently fighting for Queen and country on the Indian frontier.

Mrs Shaw observed Faro's expression and in a wide gesture which indicated the rest of the house, said, 'It is really too big for me and Barnaby and the maid. We occupy only one floor.'

An unfortunate choice of establishment in her melancholy circumstances, thought Faro, needing a whole staff of servants to keep it warm and homely.

As if she read his mind she said, 'Perhaps I should find a tenant for the upper floor and the basement.' She paused to look hard at Faro, making him wonder if she was seeking his advice. 'I might wait until things sort themselves out. At the moment, I haven't the slightest idea what the future holds,' she added with a sigh.

The baby, neglected, issued a piercing yell of indignation and Mrs Shaw rushed to pick him up. 'This is Barnaby, Inspector. Say hello, Barnaby.'

Barnaby was a fine sturdy lad, six months old. Faro knelt down. The sight and warm smell of newly-bathed baby overcame him with the nostalgia for his own now distant fatherhood.

'Hello, young fellow.' But Barnaby wasn't in the mood to be friendly and tried to obliterate himself by burrowing into his mother's shoulder. Faro was disappointed. He was fond of babies, especially good-natured ones. He had loved his two wee girls at that age. Now they were growing up away from him in Orkney, ever faster every day.

When he said so, Mrs Shaw smiled sympathetically. 'You must miss them, Inspector. Barnaby is very good, but a little shy. He doesn't see many strangers.'

'I dare say you find it lonely here.'

'Lonely?' She stared at him.

'Without your husband.'

'Oh yes. Yes, I do. Very lonely.'

'What regiment was Captain Shaw with?'

'The Caithness Regiment.'

From his mother's arms, Barnaby lunged towards Faro's watch-chain. Faro grinned, grasping the tiny starfish hand firmly. 'Got you, young fellow. I get your little game. Snatch and grab, is that it?'

Barnaby gurgled and retreated again into his mother's shoulder.

'He's a fine lad. He must be a great comfort to you.'

'Oh yes,' agreed Mrs Shaw, studying the loose thread on the baby's petticoat. A tap on the door announced the maid. 'Off you go now. Bessie will give you some milk.' She paused to plant a kiss on his forehead, then they both waved as he was whisked away, gurgling happily, by the maid.

'What about your late husband's family?'

'What about them?' she asked sharply.

'Do they see much of Barnaby?'

'Hardly. They live up north.'

'Far away?'

'Caithness.'

'That is a long way.'

'Yes.'

'Do they come often to Edinburgh?'

'Why should they?' Again her voice sounded oddly sharp, as if the question irritated her.

'They must be pleased to have such a fine handsome grandson.'

Her face softened. 'Oh yes, they are.'

A long silence followed and Faro, looking at Mrs Shaw, decided this was going to be a difficult interview. Drawing conversation promised to be what was known in Orkney as 'hard as drawing hen's teeth'.

He was puzzled by the lovely face, which should have added up to a beautiful young woman, but his first impression returned. At the Kellar's dinner party, he had mistaken that rather vacant preoccupied stare for grief. Now he wasn't quite so sure about whatever emotions, if any, she had bottled up behind that spectacular façade. What had Vince called it: Like talking to a beautiful stone statue. He wondered about those Caithness in-laws, had they disapproved of the match?

'I am anxious for news of Mabel, Inspector.'

'I was hoping you might have heard from her.'

Mrs Shaw shook her head.

'You have had no communication from her?'

She seemed surprised by the question. 'None at all. I was very shocked when Dr Kellar called to tell me that she had never been to North Berwick.'

'When did he tell you that?'

'Oh, ages ago.' She shrugged. 'More than a week. Mabel is very fond of me and, naturally, this was the very first place he came to seek her.' She paused and then said, 'It doesn't seem a bit like her, you know. Such a considerate person, not the kind who would willingly cause anyone a moment's anxiety.' She frowned. 'I wonder where on earth she can be?'

Faro decided to say nothing of the cloak and the knife at this stage. Presumably she hadn't read the newspaper.

'You have no idea what has happened to her, Inspector?'

The idea that Faro had was now almost a certainty. But he dismissed it as much too cruel and brutal to put to Mrs Kellar's 'dearest friend and companion'. A man who shied away from womanly tears at the best of times, he did not care for the prospect of dealing with a hysterical woman whose best friend has been murdered.

'I came here in the hope that she might have confided in you sometime. Mentioned friends she could be visiting . . . '

'Without telling Dr Kellar?' Mrs Shaw sounded shocked. 'She told him everything. As for pretending to go to North Berwick and then going somewhere else and staying away and frightening everyone, as I've told you, Inspector, she wasn't that sort of woman at all.'

Faro sighed deeply. There was no way of shielding her from the unpleasant truth. 'I have to tell you that Mrs Kellar's disappearance is being regarded as a very serious matter by the City Police. And if, as a close friend of hers, you know of anything, no matter how insignificant, that might shed some light on her whereabouts, then I must prevail upon you to tell me.'

Mrs Shaw frowned. 'I cannot think of a single thing that would be of any help. You know as much as I do. I am so sorry, it has been rather a waste of your time coming to me.'

'Not at all. I came at Dr Kellar's suggestion.'

Mrs Shaw coloured slightly. Her expression was fleetingly angry. 'So he told you to come here—'

Her voice rising in indignation made Faro interrupt hastily, 'We have to take everything into account, no matter how seemingly obvious or trivial.' Preparing her for what followed, he paused before adding, 'I gather from Dr Kellar that he spent part of the day that Mrs Kellar disappeared here with you. A minor detail, I'm sure, but necessary for our information.'

Confusion had overtaken anger and she hung her head. 'Mabel sometimes sends messages by him if he is to be in this area.'

'And was it a message he brought that day?'

She looked embarrassed. 'Something of the sort. Yes.'

'Could you be a little more explicit, Mrs Shaw?'

'Mabel had sent me some baby clothes for Barnaby. She is very kind to us.'

'Did Dr Kellar stay long?'

She frowned. 'About an hour or so.'

'I understand you gave him lunch and then he took you and the baby for a drive that afternoon,' Faro reminded her gently.

Mrs Shaw looked as if she was trying hard to remember. 'Yes – yes, of course.' Her second affirmative was more convincing than the first. 'Why all these questions? I know nothing of Mabel's whereabouts. As for hiding her,' she continued, her colour heightening, 'the house is yours to search, Inspector. Please go and satisfy your curiosity. There are no locked doors, only a lot of very empty rooms.'

Her voice was pathetic suddenly and Faro said assuringly, 'Please, Mrs Shaw, there is no need to upset yourself. I believe you.'

'That's a relief. You see, Mrs Kellar has been very friendly towards me, but I cannot think of one good reason why she should want to leave her own very comfortable house and take refuge in mine. Just look around you, Inspector,' she added bitterly. 'You can see how little there is here for a woman of quality.'

'I'm sorry to have wasted your time, Mrs Shaw, but we have to speak to all her friends and acquaintances. Dr Kellar is very anxious that she should be found.'

He did not add that the main purpose of his visit to check Kellar's alibi, had been successful. As he was leaving, he paused by the grand piano with its sheaves of music. 'You are to be congratulated on your playing, Mrs Shaw. It was a great pleasure, most exciting to hear your rendering of the Beethoven. I wonder, have you ever performed in public?'

'You mean on the concert platform? Oh no. I did consider it at one time, but that is rather a long story and a long time ago.'

Unless she was much older than she looked it couldn't have been all that long ago, thought Faro, suddenly curious.

'Have you thought of taking in pupils?' he asked delicately.

'I might. When Barnaby is a little older.'

Faro detected little enthusiasm for that idea. As she was showing him out, he had one more question: 'By the way, did you happen to meet anyone who knew you – any friend or neighbour – when you and Dr Kellar were out driving together two weeks ago?'

Again she coloured, this time angrily. Her eyes widened in the dawn of a new and horrifying realisation. 'You surely – you can't – you don't imagine for a moment that Dr Kellar would – would – would harm dear Mabel? The idea is preposterous. He is your police surgeon.'

As she leaned weakly against the banister, Faro felt suddenly avuncular towards the pitifully young and helplessly inadequate woman. He patted her shoulder, murmured to her not to worry, it would be all sorted out and left as sharply as politeness allowed.

As he walked swiftly down the hill overlooking the ruined and ancient Abbey and the modern railway line, Faro had a feeling that there were some curious omissions from Mrs Shaw's statements.

Her shocked realisation that Dr Kellar was under suspicion seemed genuine enough. Obviously she had no idea yet that Mabel Kellar's disappearance was being treated as murder. Of that he was certain. But he was also left with a clear impression that Mrs Shaw was not as fond of Mabel Kellar as he had first thought, or as the latter had implied during the dinner party. Eveline Shaw did not reciprocate the older woman's affection or see her in the role of 'sister of the spirit'. Doubtless she encouraged that fond illusion for the benefits that might accrue in her present unhappy situation.

Her home troubled him deeply. The absence of any

mementoes implied that Mrs Shaw was very much on her own. Was this indicative that the marriage had been against the wishes of her husband's family? And had they turned their faces away from their son's young widow and their grandchild?

Although at present Faro was aware of no motive to connect Mrs Shaw with Mabel Kellar's disappearance, his natural curiosity suggested that her present circumstances might bear further investigation.

Leaving the house, he had observed several 'For Sale' boards and that they were being negotiated through the firm of Troup and Knowles. Alex Troup was an old friend. Where better to begin a few discreet enquiries about the enigmatic Mrs Shaw?

Chapter Ten

At the Central Office, he learned that Sergeant Danny McQuinn had been assigned to help him in the Kellar enquiry. McQuinn had fallen foul of a stray bullet in a dramatic chase across the Pentland Hills and an indulgent Superintendent McIntosh had sent him to County Kerry to recuperate among his numerous relatives.

Once upon a time, Faro would have prayed that the Kellar case would be over before McQuinn returned. But he found his past antipathy dwindling. They had brought to justice several fraud cases recently and although Faro often found McQuinn obnoxious, too eager for admiration from the ladies and for promotion at all costs, he had a grudging respect for McQuinn's efficiency and recognised a detective in the making.

Nevertheless the sight of the sergeant making himself very much at home in his office during his absence revived feelings of profound irritation. It was as if McQuinn, his junior by nearly twenty years, already saw himself ousting Faro as Senior Detective Inspector. What was worse, Faro suspected that the young officer was eagerly anticipating retired – or dead man's – shoes, whichever came first in the annals of daily crime with the Edinburgh City Police.

McQuinn looked up cheekily, tapped out his pipe, removed his feet from the desk, while a grunt of disapproval from his superior officer acknowledged the exaggeratedly smart salute.

'You've recovered, I see.'

'Yes, sir. Just a flesh wound. Nothing that good old

Kerry air couldn't cure. I reported for duty this morning. Superintendent told me about our police surgeon's wife and that you might need some help. Gave me all your notes to read. An extraordinarily interesting case, Inspector, not at all what we might have expected from Dr Kellar. What was it – a brainstorm? Seems to have possibilities of an early arrest.'

'Don't know about that,' said Faro shortly. 'But you can begin with a visit to the railway station—'

'I've already been down to Waverley, talked to the porters,' interrupted McQuinn. 'No sense in waiting until you got back.'

'Find out anything?' Again Faro felt unnecessary annoyance at having his orders forestalled.

'One porter thought that a woman answering Mrs Kellar's description took the North Berwick train that morning. Very upset, in tears, he thought.'

'I've already spoken to him. The woman in question was leaving her husband and had a wee lad with her.'

'Might not have been the same woman,' said McQuinn defensively.

'That's what you're expected to find out, McQuinn. The first question you should ask is: was she alone?'

McQuinn, obviously put out at being thwarted of his first useful contribution to the enquiry, ignored the implied reprimand. He stood up, stretched lazily, flexing his shoulders.

'I thought I'd take myself off to Longniddry and have a look round there.'

Faro was scribbling a few notes. 'You might begin with some routine enquiries here. You know the sort of thing we're after. Check the Surgeons' Club. See if anyone remembers seeing him that night.'

McQuinn scanned the notes and looked across at Faro. 'This Mrs Shaw? Is she to be regarded as a suspect?'

Faro shook his head. 'Not at this stage. But I'd like to know more about her husband's family. Also when the house in Regent Crescent was purchased.'

McQuinn grinned. 'And who by, eh? Just idle curiosity, sir?'

'You should know by now that my curiosity is never idle, McQuinn,' was the stern reply.

At the door McQuinn paused. 'I don't know about you, Inspector, but something tells me there's a lot of evidence in that report of yours and nothing that really adds up worth a damn. I feel the answer might still be down at Longniddry.'

Faro's homeward journey took him close by Solomon's Tower. It stood bleak and ruinous against the skyline, dramatised by the snow-clad Salisbury Crags and Arthur's Seat. Nearly as old as the Palace of Holyroodhouse itself, Faro noticed that, as usual, its dark towers were festooned with the ragged black shapes of crows, eternally circling. Corbies, the legendary birds of ill omen; there was an element of the sinister in their hovering. What strange vigil, its reason lost in time, brought them there? What fascination lay in that domain far below, occupied by one old man and his multitude of cats?

Fighting weariness, for it had been a long day and hard walking underfoot on the packed snow, Faro decided to save a further journey by calling on Sir Hedley.

At first he thought the door was to remain unopened. When at last he heard the old man's heavy footfalls, he realised that the off-chance of Mabel Kellar's flight having taken her to this inhospitable dwelling was well beyond the bounds of credibility. Mrs Shaw had pointed out the disadvantages of Regent Crescent as a refuge, but her house represented a paradise of luxury compared to Solomon's Tower.

As within keys were turned and bolts withdrawn, the thought of stepping inside almost defeated Faro. He lingered on the doorstep. Only someone in the most desperate straits, a criminal fleeing from justice, might have run to earth, seeking shelter behind these grim grey walls. The interior smelt worse than ever and he was engulfed in a wave of cats, scampering, jumping, sliding, all in a wild rush for the fresh air, they leaped from all directions as if to escape from the dreadful odours within.

Sir Hedley's broad smile at discovering his visitor's identity revealed gums long beyond memory of teeth. 'Come in, Inspector. Most welcome, most welcome. You'll take a dram.'

Ushered along the corridor and holding his breath, Faro followed the old man into the sitting-room, thinking wryly as he did so that there was, at that moment, nothing fitting the description of 'sitting-room' available. Each seat had a cat or cats already installed, curled up and sleeping. Apart from that peaceful feline scene of somnolence, the room looked as if it had been subjected to the tender mercies of burglars, carried off by an unexpected hurricane sweeping through the house.

Faro repressed a shudder. He was by nature inclined to tidiness, except in his own study, and now he tried to avert his eyes and his nose from matters which did not concern him. His main concern was for Sir Hedley. The old man seemed far from well. His creaky breathing sounded like the turning of rusty wheels, clearly audible across the room. Occasionally rusty wheels became a deep-seated cough which seemed to emanate from the soles of his ancient boots.

Handing over a whisky glass of finest crystal but sadly in need of washing, Sir Hedley apologised, patting his chest. 'A touch of the old trouble. Lungs bad, y'know.'

Faro decided that he looked very seedy indeed. He was perspiring freely and his face had a leaden appearance.

'You look as if you're running a fever, sir. You really should see a doctor,' he said sternly.

Sir Hedley frowned. 'Thinking the same thing. Have to see someone.' Again he patted his breastbone. 'Hate doctors, can't abide them. Have to keep going though. My cats, y'know. Rely on me,' he added pathetically and giving

Faro a speculative stare. 'Thinking of calling on your young fella for advice.'

Faro thought at first that this was a joke, but Sir Hedley was in earnest.

'Took a liking to the lad. Seemed genuine. Clever too. No larking about.' He paused. 'What do you think, Inspector?'

Faro could only reply somewhat lamely, 'Of course, sir. I'll get him to come by and take a look at you.'

Sir Hedley brightened. 'Will you? Extremely good of you. Bottle is all that's needed. Clear it up in no time.' Then he laid a hand on Faro's arm. 'Be a great favour to me. A great favour.' And lifting the glass, '*Slàinte*!'

'*Slàinte*, sir!' They drank in silence.

'Suppose you're here about my niece,' said Sir Hedley.

When Faro said that was indeed the reason, the old man nodded. 'Thought so. Bad business. Bad business,' and shaking his head sadly, 'Haven't seen her since the party.'

So that was that. Faro didn't doubt for a moment that he spoke the truth. A few minutes' polite talk and then he could decently make his escape and breathe freely once more in the open air. He accepted another dram.

'When did you hear about Mrs Kellar?'

'Oh, Melville came by. Week ago. Demanding to know if I was hiding her.' His laugh changed into a deep cough. 'Used to look in sometimes. Brought me things. Food. Saw that I was all right. Kind gal.'

He stopped and gave Faro a long look. 'Can't imagine her coming here, can you? Can you?'

'Not really, sir,' said Faro uncomfortably.

'Of course not. Doesn't like cats,' added Sir Hedley in tones of righteous surprise and indignation.

'May I ask you something rather personal, sir? Did Mrs Kellar ever give you any hint that she wasn't happy?'

Sir Hedley thought about that. 'Sometimes had a feeling

that all wasn't well with Melville. Bit of a rascal, if you ask me.'

'In what way?'

'The way men are, Inspector. Women and so forth.'

'Did she confide something of the sort?'

Sir Hedley rubbed the end of his nose. 'No, never. Loyal as they come. As I said, just a feeling I had. Y'know, something wrong.'

When Faro reached home Vince was waiting for him. His first question: 'Well, any news of Mabel?'

'Nothing, lad.'

'She hasn't been to Eveline Shaw's?'

Vince listened anxiously as Faro outlined briefly his visit to Regent Crescent and his own reactions to the young widow.

'Now you understand why I found the relationship between Mabel and Eveline so extraordinary,' said Vince triumphantly. 'Your matchmaking idea was absolute nonsense.' Then, regarding his stepfather quizzically, 'Wait a minute – unless you were the lucky man?'

'You're not trying to say that Mabel was matchmaking Mrs Shaw with me. Come along, lad. Now who's talking nonsense.'

'I'm not, Stepfather. It's quite true. Now I realise how distant she was with me, how very uninterested. It's all coming back. You were the one she talked to most.'

'If that was most, it was very little. And only because I praised the Beethoven. Good Lord, Vince, I'm old enough to be her father. She's more your age than mine.'

Vince nodded and regarded Faro approvingly. 'And I hope I look as good as you do when I'm approaching forty.' When his stepfather snorted in disbelief, Vince continued sagely, 'It's true, and you know it. Be modest if you like, but you know and I know that a man who is attractive to the opposite sex is like a good wine – he only improves with the years. Besides when did age make any difference?'

'If I'm not mistaken, we seem to have had this conversation before and quite recently,' said Faro coldly.

Vince paused and grinned impishly. 'Oh yes, indeed. About a certain young miss from Canada.'*

'And we all know how that ended.'

'Well, it should have proved to you that some young ladies prefer older men.' A moment later, he asked, 'What was Eveline Shaw's late husband like, I wonder?'

'I have no idea.'

'No regimental photograph? Really, you surprise me. There's a great vogue these days for officers having a group photograph. And what about his lovely wife? Surely he would want to take her likeness on active service with him.'

'He may well have done so, but there were no mementoes of any kind. Nothing personal about the room at all, in fact. It was as if Mrs Shaw and her baby were living in a rather expensive but not very comfortable hotel.'

'How very curious. Nothing to remind her of the gallant Captain. I wonder if they had any contact or were even happy together in what must have been quite a brief marriage.'

'Considering the baby, who is a fine wee chap, they must have had contact at some time.'

'Yes, but I wonder if their communication existed outside the bedroom.' Vince thought for a moment and then asked, 'How did the stunning Mrs Shaw strike you on second meeting, Stepfather?'

'Not very much different from the first time, I'm afraid.'

'I suppose there are lots of females exactly like Eveline Shaw and perhaps some men are quite content with a beautiful package.'

'I'm sure that is the rule rather than the exception, lad.'

'I'm given to understand that we are now in danger of

* *Blood Line*

a new breed of womankind, who are no longer content to be treated as domestic slaves.'

'Aye, but most men, particularly of my generation, disapprove very strongly of such a preposterous idea. They consider that their hereditary rights, inherited from Adam, are being threatened.'

'I like the idea of this new woman, Stepfather, outrageous as it may seem. If I ever took a wife then I'd want more than a beautiful doll to undress and take to bed every night. I'd want more than begetting and procreation and stern reminders about conjugal rights.'

'Not all men are so demanding, Vince. Many just want that pretty doll who in time fulfils the functions of providing bed and board and a litter of sons and daughters.'

'Not for me, Stepfather. I believe that wives should be regarded as rather higher than breeding cattle. And if I ever find the right woman, I'd like to feel that we shared everything, the better and the worse. Especially on the intellectual plane, a sense of minds being united as well as bodies.'

'"Let me not to the marriage of true minds admit impediments",' quoted Faro.

'The Bard knew all about love, didn't he?'

'Yes, but I think the Moor of Venice probably tells us more about poor Mabel and Dr Kellar than the Sonnets.'

'True, Stepfather, sadly true. Mabel adored him and he treated her like the ground under his feet.' Vince looked thoughtful. 'Although I can't yet take in the idea of him murdering her. To me, it is still quite fantastic, beyond the bounds of belief, although I have a sneaking hope that he might be made to suffer a little bit. Teach the arrogant bastard a well-needed lesson.'

There was no way Faro could avoid telling Vince about the visit to the Kellar house and the implications of the bloodstained upholstery in the carriage.

'Oh my God,' whispered Vince, his face paling.

'It sounds bad, I know, lad. But let's not spring to

conclusions. It could have been from game he'd shot, or a rabbit, just like the maid said. If he was guilty in the way you are imagining, then don't you think he would have tried to remove the stains himself and not made a great fuss about the condition of the carriage.'

'True enough, except that he thinks of domestics as a sub-human species, incapable of the same feelings and presumably the same imagination as the rest of mortals.' Vince was silent before continuing: 'If only we could discover where those stains came from.'

'This German doctor you were telling me about? The one who is experimenting on blood types.'

'Doctor Landois. He was visiting Walter when I was in Vienna and we had a long chat. Of course, his experiments are still in the early stages, but he's quite convinced that he has made an important scientific discovery.'

Vince leaned across the table. 'When he heard that my stepfather was concerned with murder, he grew tremendously excited. Kept telling me how invaluable it would be some day in the detection of crimes. Insisted I should know what the procedure entailed. I have it written down somewhere.'

'That might come in very useful, lad, if you'd like to try it out. Not on the carriage upholstery. Too late for that but on the fur cloak.'

'I know it sounds very far-fetched, but if Landois's experiments are successful, he reckons that human blood also falls into several different groups and that it is completely different from the composition of animal blood.'

'If your doctor is right and blood differs from one human being to another, then this could open a new phase for the police,' said Faro excitedly.

'I've been thinking along life-giving lines rather than the hangman's rope,' said Vince drily. 'The transfusion of blood from one human to another could save a patient's life. Someone who has lost a lot of blood in an accident, or a woman in childbirth. We encounter this every day and we just have to stand back and helplessly watch them just bleed to death.'

'It's a fascinating theory, Vince. Let's hope there's something in it.'

'Perhaps I could have a look at poor Mabel's cloak?'

'And the knife too. Although I'd better warn you, what we might call the evidence has been diluted by lying under the snow for a couple of weeks.'

'If they were wrapped up, as you say, then I think there'll be enough remaining to give some interesting results.'

'I hope you're right.'

'Do you realise, Stepfather, that in the normal way, this would become the province of the police surgeon.'

'In these circumstances,' said Faro hastily, 'I think it would be advisable to bypass the good doctor.'

'How did he react to the bloodstained brougham?'

'Too late to tackle him on that, but I dare say he'd have some glib explanation.'

'I've just remembered something, Stepfather. On two occasions when I had luncheon with Mabel, Kellar had been out shooting for the pot. She was very proud of his marksmanship. Didn't seem to regard it as a curious choice of leisure pursuit for a man who spends his time up to the elbows in blood almost every day.'

He gave a shudder of distaste. 'Frankly, though, I can't see Dr Kellar coming home in his carriage from Surgeons Hall dripping blood anyway. He always leaves well-scrubbed. Although some doctors are careless about such things and don't bother, Kellar is most meticulous. You wouldn't find him wearing his butcher's apron, as they call it, outside the dissecting room.'

As Mrs Brook came in with the supper, Faro reminded Vince about the Beethoven concert at the Assembly Rooms. 'It's Hallé conducting and the divine Neruda playing the Beethoven violin concerto.'

'Oh, Stepfather. I can't. It's Rob's twenty-first and there's a celebration arranged. I am sorry.'

'Oh, don't worry about it, lad. I dare say I'll find someone at the Central Office to accompany me.' But Faro doubted that. His taste in music was considered a little bizarre.

Instead of being content with promenading in Princes Street Gardens and listening, or rather only half-listening, above the constant chatter, to the military brass bands, Faro parted with a precious shilling for the luxury of sitting down in the Assembly Rooms and listening with rapt attention to a full orchestra. He knew that such activity caused much whispered comment among his colleagues. They regarded frequenting concert halls as a recreation belonging to the higher strata of Edinburgh society and, as such, not quite the thing for a detective inspector.

'How are the rest of your enquiries going, Stepfather? Where next?'

'I called in at Solomon's Tower.'

'Ah, my favourite suspect.' Vince's grimace warned Faro that he was not going to be greatly impressed at having to set foot in Solomon's Tower to examine Sir Hedley as a patient.

Faro was right and Vince swore.

'Sorry, lad, I let you in for it.'

'I suppose such a challenge is good for my soul. Having to remember the Hippocratic Oath and all that sort of thing. Even when wicked old devils are concerned.'

'Look, you make up a bottle of medicine for his cough and I'll hand it in, explaining that you're busy.'

'Oh no, you won't, Stepfather. It's good of you to offer but very soon seeing patients is going to be my daily bread. I can't afford to be choosy and whether I love them or hate them will be a matter of total indifference. All my concern will be trying to make a damned good job of curing them. I dare say I'll get many just as offensive – worse, although I doubt that's possible, than I find the Mad Bart.'

He grinned. 'This will be a good first lesson in humility and I might as well get used to it. Besides, I'd feel terrible, knowing he's ill, if he died and I hadn't had a look at him.'

Once again Faro found Vince's attitude to the old man, without rhyme or reason, very hard to understand.

'Just natural antipathy to the ruling classes. And the fact I can never forget or overlook that I am some nobleman's by-blow. The enormity of such injustice,' he continued bitterly, 'that I should have had aristocratic birth. Gates of privilege that were closed upon my mother and myself for ever. And what my poor mother suffered. I care more about her deprivation than my own.'

Faro didn't answer. Vince had never stopped to think whether his poor mother was fitted by her own humble upbringing to step into the role of a nobleman's wife. Lizzie hadn't often talked to Faro about the past after the early days of their marriage when she said, 'Once a servant, always a servant. I would never be able to enjoy myself, thinking about washing the dishes and clearing up after the guests had gone.'

'Come now, Stepfather, be honest. Wouldn't you feel the same if you were me?' Vince demanded.

'I don't know much about noble blood, lad. I'm of good solid farming stock as far back as any of the family can remember.'

'Only as far as Lord Robert Stuart and his Royal bastards.'

Faro laughed. 'Everyone in Orkney claims descent from Mary Queen of Scots' wicked half-brother. Rather too distant to get bitter about, don't you think? Just another romantic myth.'

'Myth or no, I'd much rather be a poor peasant and have some respectable humble ploughman for a father, or a man like you, Stepfather,' he added softly, 'who loved my mother and married her, even if she did have a bastard son. She was used so cruelly, not even allowed the romantic illusion of love. The brutal savagery of rape begot me, let us never forget that.'

Suddenly he stretched his hand across the table, smiled tenderly. 'I'm an ungrateful beast. All this prattle about an aristocratic life. We might both have been utterly miserable.

After all, Mother would never have met you and neither would I.'

He paused and smiled. 'And I have you to thank for giving us both such a truly happy home life, Stepfather. The fact that you could rise above regarding my mother as a scarlet woman, a social outcast. That was wonderful, but then, Stepfather, that's what you are.'

'Oh come, lad,' said Faro uncomfortably. 'It wasn't just one way, you know. You turned out to be a fine son.' He shook his head sadly. 'The best a father could have, thank God.'

And turning the subject on to a lighter vein, he added teasingly, 'I haven't noticed you exactly avoiding the rich life when it comes your way.'

'Not at all. Some of my best college friends are rich and bone idle and I number a couple of baronets among them. I have nothing against the rich life, if you're lucky enough to land in it. But as I'm doomed to be for ever on the other side of the fence, I intend to succeed, prove to the world that I can rise above my bastard birth.'

Chapter Eleven

Despite Vince's conjectures, the lack of any real motive for Mabel Kellar's murder continued to trouble Faro. What had Kellar to gain? He did not have long to wait for an answer. Mrs Brook brought him up a card as he was about to leave for the Central Office.

'A Mrs Findlay-Cupar wishes to see you, Inspector. I've put her in the drawing-room.' The housekeeper's hushed voice and deferential manner suggested that the Inspector need have no fears. This was quality, a 'real' lady.

'Mrs Findlay-Cupar.' As Faro took the hand of Mabel Kellar's sister, he realised the cruelty of fate that distributed astonishing good looks to one sister and none at all to the other. Laetitia Findlay-Cupar and Mabel Kellar were alike as sisters, their features almost identical. And there all similarity ended, for poor Mabel's pale colouring, lacklustre eyes and hair had been a faded watercolour, a mocking travesty of the vividly attractive woman before him.

'Forgive me calling on you informally, Inspector. My reason will be made clear directly. I won't beat about the bush. I have received news that may have some bearing on my sister's disappearance.'

Taking the seat he offered, she smiled. 'Mabel talked a great deal about your stepson and he talked to her, I understand, a great deal about you.'

'I had the pleasure of meeting your sister, ma'am. On the night before she er, left, there was a dinner party at the Grange.'

Mrs Findlay-Cupar brightened. 'Oh, that is such a help.

It makes the favour I have to ask so much easier.' Pausing, she searched his countenance anxiously and then taking a deep breath, said, 'Inspector Faro, I am taking the liberty of asking if you would personally take on this case.'

'I am already doing so, ma'am.'

Mrs Findlay-Cupar looked first relieved and then afraid. 'Dare I ask you to tell me then, quite frankly, if you have the least notion where she is or what has become of her?' Her voice dropped to a whisper. 'Is she still alive and well?'

'We are making exhaustive enquiries, ma'am.' Faro hoped he was succeeding in expressing those reassurances he was far from feeling. 'Dr Kellar asked us to investigate immediately and we are inclined to take cases of missing persons very seriously.'

Mabel's sister leaned back in her chair. 'Oh, so he asked you. That is interesting.' She sat up again hastily and withdrew an envelope from her reticule. Frowning indecisively, she tapped it against the chair's arm.

'I think you ought to know, Inspector, that all was not well with my sister, there was something troubling her deeply. When I spent a few days at the Grange recently she was very tearful.'

'How recent was this?'

'Between Christmas and New Year. At first I thought it was because she was having problems finding a new housekeeper. Dr Kellar had been very disagreeable and they had lost a very valued old servant.'

'Yes, there were some problems at the dinner party. I gather from the new housekeeper that Dr Kellar is not the easiest of employers,' said Faro.

This visit from Mabel's sister was most opportune, he thought, having already made a shrewd assessment of the woman before him. She was eager to talk and the more hooks he threw in her direction the bigger fish he might land.

'Dr Kellar has always been a very difficult man to live with but, amazingly, Mabel could find no fault in him. After twenty years of marriage, she still blindly adores him.'

Her mocking expression indicated that she found this astonishing. 'It is such a pity she never had a child. There was going to be a baby, but it came to nothing. I'm afraid that Dr Kellar disliked children intensely. He was not enamoured at the prospect of being a father and persuaded her that it would be in their best interests to remain childless . . . '

'May I ask you, was there good reason for his decision?'

'Good reason? You mean family traits, insanity and so forth.' She looked at him narrowly. 'Oh Inspector, I can see that you are thinking of our uncle. Well, his family have always had the reputation, well-earned alas, of being a fairly disreputable lot and Uncle Hedley disassociated himself with them long ago. I can assure you they have got all their wits about them. And Uncle Hedley too. But we are related only through marriage.'

She laughed. 'As for myself, I've had eight children and they are all fine in wind and limb. Mabel and I were the youngest of thirteen.' She sighed. 'No, it was nothing like that influenced Melville.'

'Could there have been something in his side of the family?'

'The Kellars have been respected in Edinburgh for many generations.' She smiled. 'I imagine your police are fully aware of their police surgeon's impeccable background. Besides people who love each other and want children desperately will always believe in God's goodness, that in their case the worst won't happen.'

There was a rather long silence as if Mrs Findlay-Cupar was reliving Mabel's unhappiness, before she resumed. 'Over the years, apart from the unhappy business over the baby, I have always found Mabel loyal and uncomplaining, quite content and happy in her life. She was a dutiful obedient wife and she readily came to terms with her husband's wishes in every respect, even to remaining childless.

'Yes, I would have said she was happy with Melville. Until very recently.' Again she looked away from him, cautious, hesitant. 'When I last saw her she was very upset, prone to tears on the least provocation. I had never seen her in such a state. It seemed, Inspector, that she had reason to believe that her beloved Melville was being unfaithful to her.'

And a pity it was that she had ever found out at all, thought Faro grimly. He was one of many at the Central Office who entertained shrewd suspicions that Kellar would not restrict his amorous activities to one rather plain prim wife.

Kellar was a handsome man who basked in female adulation and, like many professional men, found that opportunities for infidelity often came his way. He could afford extra-marital relations carried on with utmost discretion. Apparently this time he hadn't been clever or discreet enough.

As if she read Faro's thoughts, Mrs Findlay-Cupar continued, 'I tried to assure her that this was nonsense, and even if it wasn't nonsense, men like Melville do not risk scandal by leaving their wives for other women. I said all the things expected in the way of comfort from one sister to another. Bear with it, be patient, it will pass and so forth.'

She thrust the letter towards him almost reluctantly. 'This came from my sister. It was deposited with our family solicitor with instructions that unless he heard from her to the contrary this was to be delivered to me at North Berwick on February 4th. As February 5th is my fortieth birthday, and Mabel is always extremely generous, I presumed that this was some gift of bonds, a legacy of some kind. Please read it, Inspector.' She smiled wanly. 'Tiz is my pet name.'

My dearest Tiz: I write to you because I am at the end of my tether. I have found out something so awful I can hardly bring myself to believe it or put it into words. I was right – there is another woman.

Melville whom I love with all my heart, whom I have trusted with all my being, has a mistress. I have definite proof of this – they have been seen together. What is worse, I know her. Not only is she his mistress but there is a child. His child, whom he dotes upon.

Dearest Tiz, I am in agony. He has asked me to leave this house – my only home – as he no longer has any use for me. He no longer wants me for his wife. Our marriage is over but I am to say nothing, he says, until the knighthood is safe, otherwise it will be the worse for me. Dearest Tiz, what am I to do? I love him – love him – he is my whole life, but my life is in his hands and I fear that if I don't agree to his wishes that he will do away with me. Once he gets an idea nothing – nobody – is ever allowed to stand in his way.

What he really wants now is to marry this woman and legitimise their child. Everything is for the child, this bastard he worships. His only talk is about securing his son's future. I think I could share him with a mistress, bear with the ignominy as I know so many other wives do, if only he had let me keep our baby, then there would have been some comfort. But now I have nothing, no one to turn to.

I think if I do not agree then he will kill me. Do not laugh, dearest Tiz, he could dispose of me so easily, so cruelly and he has told me so many times, even laughing, how easy murder would be for a police surgeon. And I would rather he cut out my heart, the heart that is and always will be his, rather than live without him.

Your heartbroken sister, Mabel.

P.S.: You may never receive this letter. I trust not. On the other hand, it and I may arrive on your doorstep without warning and, knowing the state of mind I will be in by then, I should like you to be in possession of a more articulate version of the true facts.

Faro laid it aside. A heartrending, moving letter, written in haste and desperation. Some words were almost illegible, blotted and smudged by her tears. But it was the words heavily underlined that troubled him most, with their appalling significance, as if Mabel Kellar had indeed a premonition of the dreadful fate that lay in store for her.

Mrs Findlay-Cupar declined to take it back. 'Keep it, Inspector. I know I can rely on your discretion. And if Dr Kellar has indeed put away my dearest sister, then I want him brought to justice. And if this letter will help to put a rope around his neck, then let it be done.'

'One thing puzzles me,' said Faro. 'The baby Mrs Kellar mentions, that she wasn't allowed to keep. I'm not sure that I understand.'

'I'm not sure that I do either,' said Mrs Findlay-Cupar hurriedly. 'I believe that Melville with his medical knowledge could have averted a threatened miscarriage, but declined to do so.'

'I see. Your sister's statement does rather imply that the baby was born alive and then put out for adoption.'

'You have my assurance, Inspector, there was no child.'

Faro saw her into her carriage. She thanked him for receiving her so informally and he promised to keep her in touch with any events relating to Mabel Kellar.

Vince was waiting for him. 'Well, what news of Mabel?'

Faro handed him the letter.

Vince could hardly control his emotion as he read, his face grew pale with horror. 'This is utterly appalling, Stepfather, appalling. The man is an absolute devil. This letter proves without a shadow of doubt that he planned to get rid of Mabel. It's all there in her own words, Stepfather. Why don't you go and arrest him?'

'It certainly provides a new and damning aspect of

the case against Kellar, lad, but without further evidence a court of law would dismiss it as the hysterical denunciations of a betrayed wife.'

'What about Mabel's bloodstained fur cloak, and the knife? What further proof do you need to put a rope around Kellar's neck?' demanded Vince angrily.

'A body,' said Faro shortly.

Vince shuddered and gave him an angry look. 'At least you are wrong about your motive this time, Stepfather. This hardly fits into your pet theory of gain.'

'That rather depends, lad. There are many aspects of gain and in this case it would appear that Kellar realised, almost too late, the benefits of fatherhood.'

'Of a bastard son,' said Vince bitterly. 'One that he wanted so desperately that he was prepared to go to any lengths, even murder, to legitimise.'

'Thereby following the desperate example of kings and nobles who set the pattern in ancient times and got rid of inconveniently barren wives.'

'Like Henry the Eighth?'

'If succession and a throne are in jeopardy then history is prepared to turn a blinder eye than Edinburgh society. I'm afraid as far as Kellar is concerned the scandal of divorce would have ruined him.'

Faro was silent, deep in thought. Have I been expecting something like this? Was this damning document written by a frightened wife the missing piece of the puzzle? Once you have that, the complete picture springs into view and leaves you wondering why on earth you hadn't seen the strikingly obvious.

'I wonder,' he said.

'You surely can't have any further doubts that Kellar is guilty after this. There were plenty of veiled hints among the students that the ladies pursued Kellar and that he wasn't averse to walking slowly.'

Faro smiled. Even the shrewd Sir Hedley Marsh had hinted that Melville was a womaniser.

While they were talking Faro had been mulling over the contents of the letter and had come to a rather obvious but very disturbing conclusion regarding the unknown woman's identity.

In reply to his question, Vince shook his head. 'No, Mabel never even hinted to me that she suspected Kellar of philandering. Misplaced loyalty, I suppose.'

'To whom?' demanded Faro sharply.

'Why, to her husband, of course.' He thought for a moment. 'I expect it was the kind of topic she considered too indelicate to discuss with a man. It never occurred to me to ask, but now that you mention it, she might well have confided in her best friend. Mrs Shaw, for instance.'

'Ah yes, Mrs Shaw. I've been thinking about her. A young woman with an infant. A son,' he added heavily. 'Does that not strike you as a remarkable coincidence?'

Vince stared at him indignantly. 'It strikes me as absolute sheer coincidence, Stepfather. And that's all. Mrs Shaw is a respectable widow. Why, Stepfather, I'm surprised at you even entertaining such a notion. You surely can't be seriously implying that Eveline Shaw would have an – an affair – with her best friend's husband? After all Mabel's kindness to her?'

'It has been known,' said Faro drily.

'But in this case, you should know better. You have the evidence of your own eyes. You saw them at the dinner party.'

One of Faro's lasting impressions had been Mrs Kellar's apparent devotion, her many smiles and anxiety that Mrs Shaw be included in every conversation, often staring uneasily at Kellar who was barely civil to the young woman.

'I'm just speaking my thoughts out loud,' said Faro. And tactfully changing the subject, 'When did you first become friendly with Mrs Kellar?'

'About three months ago, but it seems as if I've known her for a lifetime.'

'I'm curious about this baby she wasn't allowed to keep? Did she ever mention it to you?'

'Not on that occasion,' said Vince hurriedly. 'I was collecting some papers for Kellar and she asked for my advice on a quite minor affliction, some stiffness in her shoulder. As it turned out a pulled muscle, but she was worried that this might be the onset of rheumatism, common in her family.

'While I was examining her I observed a considerable amount of bruising. The nature and positions were curious and suggested that she had been physically beaten. She made several transparent excuses, but her reluctance became obvious.'

Vince fell silent and Faro said, 'Her assailant was none other than her own husband, was that it?'

Vince nodded. 'You guessed right, Stepfather. I was shocked and furious, although I knew Kellar to be a man quite capable of fits of sarcasm and even cold anger with his students. Anyway,' he continued, 'poor Mabel was full of blushing whispers and tears of embarrassment, trying to excuse her husband's ill-treatment. I was desperately sorry for her but, what was worse, I was quite helpless. Without betraying Mabel's confidence and making it a lot worse for her, I couldn't confront him with his beastly behaviour, tell him – my superior, my employer – to desist and that he was several kinds of swine.'

Vince banged down his glass on the table. 'Dear God. I shouldn't even be telling you all this, Stepfather, such matters between patient and doctor are utterly sacrosanct.'

'Quite so. Doctors are like priests in being the recipients of intimate confidences. I'm fully aware of that and you can rely on my discretion.'

'I am only telling you,' Vince continued desperately, 'because the matter is one of life – and I think, dear God, death too. And you, most of all, you must understand the sort of beast you are dealing with.'

Faro regarded his stepson with compassion. Vince might

be shocked by Mabel's revelations, but Faro could have reiterated many such tales of respectable middle-class men who allied Christian virtue with hypocrisy and abused their wives, treating them little better than animals once the bedroom door was closed. Faro knew of many husbands who could get no pleasure from normal lovemaking and sought satisfaction in outlandish and even brutish practices.

'His treatment of her was the first bond between us,' Vince whispered. 'I was, it seemed, as a doctor who was also a friend, the only person she could confide in.'

'What about Mrs Shaw?'

Vince gave him a sharp look. 'I think not. Mabel would have been too embarrassed and humiliated to confess such matters to another woman, especially one so much younger.'

Faro rubbed his chin thoughtfully. 'Has it ever occurred to you that as there were no children, you would be about the right age as a substitute for the son she had never had.'

Vince laughed. 'You imagine that that was the reason for us being drawn to each other.' He shook his head. 'Not so, Stepfather. You are wrong this time. Far from it. And her confessions, I assure you, were hardly the sort a mother would make to her son.'

'She told you the reason there were no children to the marriage?'

'She did indeed,' said Vince grimly.

Faro waited a moment and then said, 'Well, what were they?'

Vince looked doubtful, and regarded his stepfather uneasily. 'I don't know that I really ought to tell you, Stepfather. It is not a pretty story and one, I must warn you, which will only further prejudice you against Kellar.'

'I will have to take that chance.' When Vince hesitated, Faro continued, 'Come, come, lad. There is, and always has been, a tendency for husband to blame wife when the fault is not hers at all. You must know as a doctor, surely, that a man's pride suffers a mortal blow when he realises that his manhood is incapable of begetting a child.'

Vince remained silent and Faro said. 'You had better tell me. What was it? Syphilis? There couldn't be anything much worse.'

'Oh yes, there could. There could indeed.'

'Such as?'

'Aborting one's own wife.'

Faro stared at him. 'You don't mean . . . '

'I do mean. That the beast Kellar never wanted a child and refused to let his wife conceive. He took elaborate precautions, so she told me, and when by accident – or design, poor soul, since she yearned for a child – she became pregnant, he coldly insisted that the foetus be aborted.'

Faro shuddered. 'Dreadful. I can hardly believe that any husband would be so callous, so inhuman. There must have been some very good reason for such a terrible decision. A father-to-be often suffers qualms of conscience, such as fearing that he is too poor, or the world a too wicked place, to entrust another life into it.'

'Such reasoning could hardly be valid in Kellar's case, with so much to offer a child.'

'He might have feared taking second place in his wife's affections.'

Vince laughed derisively. 'An unlikely story. You've seen them together. You don't really believe that, do you?'

Faro remembered his own qualms when Rose was conceived within weeks of his marriage to Lizzie. He had felt dread and resentment of being plunged into fatherhood before they had a chance to get to know each other. 'There is always that other fear, that the mother may not survive childbirth.'

Such had been Lizzie Faro's fate with their third child. The two men, her husband and her beloved firstborn, exchanged stricken glances. Vince stretched over and put his hand on Faro's arm. 'You must not torment yourself, Stepfather. You were not to blame. Mother so wanted to give you a son.'

Faro patted his hand. 'I know, lad, I know. But nevertheless . . . ' Blinking away tears, he said, 'Oh, let's get back to Kellar. Presumably at that time he loved Mabel, so there must have been some other reason for his decision.'

'There was none. Only his detestation of children, which must have made Mabel's agony even harder to bear when she wrote to her sister.'

'This does indeed throw another light on her letter,' said Faro 'How appalling.'

'It was indeed. Can you imagine the feelings of a woman whose husband had put her through the depths of hell, both physically and mentally. That would be bad enough, except that when she is beyond child-bearing, he cheerfully gets his young mistress pregnant. And, worst of all, he dotes upon her child and wants to claim it as his own.'

Vince stared at him with stricken eyes. 'Dear God, don't you see how monstrous and inhuman Kellar is?'

'Aye, lad. I do. I'm shocked too. In the class Kellar belongs to, fathers need play little part in the upbringing beyond the begetting. Once property and inheritance are settled, the offspring can be safely left to the tender mercies of nurses and public schools.'

'Yes, however we look at it, an heir is often the only reason for marrying at all. As I fear it will be mine,' said Vince. 'But not until I am very old.'

Faro smiled. Vince's fierce determination to remain a bachelor was a constant source of discussion and friendly argument between them.

'Well, Stepfather, would you not say that this was the first indication of a black-hearted murderer?'

Faro shook his head. 'I can't believe that Kellar could have aborted his own child without extenuating circumstance, some powerful reason.'

'Some dread medical history in his wife's family which

he wanted to spare her, like insanity, is that what you are suggesting?' said Vince.

'We have her sister's assurances on that. From the standpoint of eight healthy children.'

'And the Mad Bart is only a relative by marriage, unfortunately,' said Vince.

'Aye, lad. And despite his nickname he's as sane as the next man. A recluse, with his own reasons for withdrawing from society.'

'Eccentric, crafty and wicked, I don't doubt, but sharp as a tack.' Vince jumped up from the table and strode over to the window, staring at the winter sunlight dying on Arthur's Seat.

'The story isn't quite over yet, Stepfather. Prepare yourself for something worse, much worse. And I doubt that even you will find excuses for Kellar's inhumanity.' Taking a deep breath he continued. 'Not only did this vile man remove the foetus conceived by himself upon his wife, he used it for experiments.'

Slamming his fists together, he turned to Faro. 'Experiments, Stepfather. You know what that means, cutting to pieces, coldly dissecting his own unborn daughter.'

'A daughter? It was so far advanced.'

'Yes. Mabel told me so. A female child. A female child who would have been about the same age as Eveline Shaw.'

Eveline Shaw.

Both men were silent and then Faro asked, 'Are there any other young women with babies in the Kellar circle?'

'They didn't have a social circle, Stepfather. I think I knew most of their acquaintances – yes, I'd call them that.'

'Considering that Mrs Kellar was so forthright about her husband's brutish treatment, I should have thought his infidelity would have been worth a mention. I'm surprised she gave no hint of it.'

'You're going too fast, Stepfather. You have the answer

there before you. Read her letter again. She had suffered the last fatal blow to that cherished illusion she had kept alive through their marriage. That Kellar still loved her in his fashion. Don't you see, a woman like Mabel had her pride. She could uncomplainingly endure and suffer physical ill-usage far more readily than her husband's adultery.'

Chapter Twelve

The revelations about Mabel Kellar's life with her husband were appalling, and although his stepson prided himself on being Mabel's confidant, Faro was in little doubt as to the identity of Kellar's mistress. He decided that an informal call on Mrs Shaw might prove worthwhile, especially as the bait he had to offer as excuse for the visit, was calculated to gain her confidence and promote further agreeable and sympathetic acquaintance.

When Vince asked if he had found a companion for the Neruda concert, Faro said, 'I've decided to ask Mrs Shaw to accompany me.'

'Mrs Shaw? Good heavens. Well, well.'

'As you're so fond of quoting, lad, music sounds ten times better when it is being shared by someone of a harmonious disposition. In this case who better than Mrs Shaw?' Watching his stepson's mocking expression, Faro's icy glare forbade the usual teasing.

'And I'll have none of your innuendos, if you please. The concert serves a double purpose since it provides an admirable opportunity of continuing my investigations. Discreetly, of course.'

'Of course, Stepfather.'

Vince's unchanging smile mocked him and he added angrily, 'Dammit, you know my feelings about her.'

'Ah yes, that is all very well, but do we know her feelings about you?'

'Listen to me,' said Faro heatedly, 'Even without the business about Mabel Kellar, I would still feel sorry for a young widow. Especially a talented pianist with possibly few chances to attend concerts or to hear the divine Neruda play. So it's a bit early in the day for you to start hearing wedding bells, I must say,' he added huffily.

'All right, Stepfather, I stand corrected and I apologise.' Vince's impudent grin was anything but apologetic, 'You're very sure of yourself where the ladies are concerned, so let's hope it stays that way and that one day I don't have to remind you with "I told you so".' He stretched out his hand, 'May I see that letter again?' And examining it carefully, 'You have observed that it is un-dated.'

Faro nodded. 'Irritating, isn't it?'

'But hardly surprising, considering poor Mabel's state of mind when it was written. Did Tiz leave you the envelope?'

'Here it is.'

'No postmark?'

'The answer is that the contents were too important to entrust to the mail or to any other person and Mrs Kellar most likely handed in to the solicitor's office personally.'

'When? Hardly on the way to the station without attracting Kellar's curiosity. Do you see what I'm getting at, Stepfather? The dinner party was on Sunday, so if Eveline Shaw was Kellar's mistress, Mabel already knew.' Vince jabbed a finger at him. 'Which makes absolute nonsense of your theory, doesn't it? You just have to remember her behaviour that evening,' he laughed. 'Mabel would need to be a far better actress than I credit her for to have sustained that elaborate exhibition of devotion to her dearest friend and companion. It has to be someone else, Stepfather. It can't be Eveline Shaw.'

The afternoon was bright and cheerful, with a cloudless frosty sky stretching to infinity. An azure glow hung over the Castle, a great sleeping stone monster dwarfing the ant-like creatures who scuttled back and forth along Princes Street enjoying the brief respite of springtime promise. Crouched among its own dark secrets, so the Castle had stood through centuries of winter snow and summer sunshine, a silent witness impervious to man's follies, his despairs and fleeting triumphs.

Faro's thoughts turned to the interview that lay ahead. Vince's argument failed to convince him, despite Mrs Kellar's display of affection to Mrs Shaw at the dinner party. Regardless of when that damning letter had been delivered to the solicitor's office, he had not the slightest doubt that Mrs Shaw was Kellar's mistress and that Barnaby was his son.

He saw that public façade of indifference and even dislike for what it was: a ruse, imperative if their association was to remain a closely-guarded secret. The whole evening must have been torture for them both, especially for Mrs Shaw. This theory interpreted her vaguely distressed manner, not as carrying a still inconsolable burden of grief for her dead husband but as constant terror that by word or glance her intimate relationship with Melville Kellar might be made apparent to Mabel.

Was it possible that Mrs Kellar had been naive enough to imagine that her sweet and caring behaviour would stir some pangs of conscience in the guilty pair and that Eveline Shaw, in particular, might decide to end the affair? If Mabel Kellar thought along such lines, Faro decided grimly, then she had a pitiful grasp of human nature or the fact that love, once dead, was seldom resurrected by self-sacrifice.

Faro was pleased with his astute observation that from Mrs Shaw's viewpoint the devoted friendship was somewhat one-sided. It did not take much imagination to realise that the young woman must be desperate to give Barnaby a father. And since Kellar was eager to bestow the benefits of parenthood on his bastard son, the presence of a legal wife was very inconvenient.

It was also the perfect motive for murder.

The day's pale warmth was deceptive and Faro reached Mrs Shaw's house half-frozen. Head down against the chill wind blowing straight off the Firth of Forth, he almost cannoned into the young man who was dashing down her front steps, having banged the door with shattering force behind him. A lightly built young man of middle height, with the darkly handsome looks of the Celtic Highlander, he was in a high old temper. Face flushed and distorted with rage, he swept past Faro, unseeing and without apology.

Behind him, the door that had been so forcefully closed opened to reveal Mrs Shaw, breathless and distraught. Faro realised that she must have rushed downstairs in the wake of the departed visitor. Tear-stained, her expression of anticipation changed into deepest melancholy when she beheld Detective Inspector Faro standing on her doorstep, instead of the young man beseeching her forgiveness with abject apologies.

Faro raised his hat, bowed. 'Good day to you, ma'am.'

Mrs Shaw summoned a smile, looking bleakly beyond him down the now empty street.

I couldn't have chosen a less inauspicious moment to call and invite her to a concert, thought Faro, expecting an abrupt refusal.

But Mrs Shaw had regained her equilibrium and saw his visit in quite another light. 'Is it about Mabel?' she asked anxiously.

Faro had to confess, no, it wasn't.

Mrs Shaw frowned. 'I was hoping you had news of her at last. Such a long time. I wonder where on earth she can be?'

'I'm sure we'll find her,' said Faro smoothly, listening to his own false tone offering consolation where he was certain there was none. 'It was quite another matter brought me to your door this time.'

Her eyes, deeply violet, opened wide. Surprise became her exceedingly well, he thought, a very pretty sight indeed. 'I wondered if you would like to go to the concert this evening. Neruda is playing the Beethoven Violin Concerto.'

Mrs Shaw didn't seem to hear him. 'I beg your pardon?'

He repeated the request and this time she stood very still. Her attitude of careful concentration and growing amazement suggested that a Detective Inspector was the last person from whom she expected such an invitation.

'My stepson usually accompanies me but he is engaged elsewhere,' Faro said, feeling that explanation was necessary. 'And knowing your interest in Beethoven . . . ' How lame it all sounded! He had wasted his time. He shouldn't have come, made a fool of himself.

But she was smiling. 'Oh, thank you. I would be delighted.' She clasped her hands together like an eager child given a particular treat. 'I would love that. Oh, I do thank you, Inspector.'

There was an awkward pause while she gazed at him, wondering what to say next while Faro considered whether he should take his leave before she changed her mind.

Smiling, as if she had come to a sudden decision, she opened the door a little wider. 'It's very cold standing on the doorstep. Barnaby is out with the girl, but they'll be back shortly. Would you care to come inside, take some refreshment?'

'Only if I could prevail upon you to play the Appassionata again,' said Faro wistfully.

Her answering smile was shy but happy. 'If that would give you pleasure, of course I will.'

He followed her up to the bare drawing-room and she sat down immediately at the piano. As she struck the first chords, again Faro had the feeling that he was listening to the true artist, the musician who was no longer conscious of him, of the room or, beyond the room, of time itself.

As he listened, rapt by her playing, he was no longer concerned that Eveline Shaw might be an accessory to murder. With her he too escaped into that boundless enchanted world of the senses. As the last liquid tones faded into silence, she sat with her fingers still on the keys, head downbent, unwilling to make that transition back into painful everyday existence with all its attendant cares.

Faro's applause, his whispered 'Bravo, bravo' seemed almost an intrusion and it coincided with jarring reality in the form of screams of rage. Growing ever nearer and more ear-piercing, they took form as a scarlet-faced, square-mouthed monster, hardly recognisable as the once genial baby Barnaby, was carried across the threshold by a frantic maid.

'Sorry, ma'am, I canna' be dealing wi' him today. Real naughty he is. Just had to bring him home.'

Mrs Shaw rushed to the rescue, seized those waving, clenched fists. 'Oh bad, bad Barnaby. Is it your teeth again, my precious?'

Faro found himself now examining the baby for likeness to Melville Kellar. Certainly the passion of rage before him struck a chord of familiarity. But the baby's continued screams put firmly at an end any immediate possibility of further conversation, or of putting into effect his own subtle methods of trapping suspects into betraying incriminating evidence.

His eardrums were sorely afflicted by the din, which threatened to be prolonged and immediate withdrawal seemed prudent. Indicating his intention, he called, 'Tonight at seven,' to which a harassed Mrs Shaw looked over her shoulder and shouted above the tumult, 'I will be ready. Thank you.' And to the maid, 'Please see the Inspector out.'

Faro gladly made his escape, the divine music of Beethoven and the baby's angry yells jostling each other in his head. Annoyed that the visit had been cut short without the least advantage to his enquiries, he was not the man to accept the frustrations of questions unanswered where such information could be readily obtained.

His way back to the Central Office took him past the rooms of Mrs Kellar's solicitors. Shown the envelope, the clerk at the desk looked through his register and shook his head. 'As this was marked private and personal, it would be taken directly to Mr Franklin and would not be entered.

I cannot give you any further details,' he added severely. 'You will need to approach Mr Franklin himself on the subject and he is in Court at Dundee today.'

Making a note to send McQuinn to interview Mr Franklin next day, Faro walked a little further along to Hanover Street and entered the office of Mr Alex Troup. He found that gentleman seated at his desk behind a mountain of documents. Always glad for a chat about hectic events the two had shared in Faro's earlier days with the City Police, he greeted his old friend warmly.

After a few solicitous enquiries on the well-being of Faro's mother and his two small daughters in Orkney, Alex Troup regarded him quizzically. 'I gather this isn't a social call, Jeremy. Is there something I can do for you?'

'There is indeed.'

When Faro explained that he wanted the name of the buyer of Mrs Shaw's house, Alex Troup regarded him sternly. 'You know, of course, that request is highly irregular. Such information is confidential but your visit implies that this is police business?'

'Yes. A murder investigation.'

Alex Troup went immediately to his files. A moment later he emerged, document in hand. 'Mrs Eveline Shaw. The house was purchased in the name of Dr Melville Kellar.'

Faro felt the glow of triumph. He had been right. 'And the date?'

'July of last year.'

'You've been a tremendous help, Alex.'

The date of purchase confirmed all he needed to know. This information was too significant to be written off as coincidence. Kellar had set up Eveline Shaw in the house in Regent Crescent when the son she had borne him was a few weeks old.

Returning to the Central Office, the report of a break-in at a Princes Street store and the round-up of suspected villains from the notorious Wormwoodhall was to command

Inspector Faro's full attention until early evening, driving out all thoughts of the evening ahead.

At last, he left matters in McQuinn's hands and hurried back to Sheridan Place. Vince had yet not arrived home for supper to be regaled with the new developments.

Fearing he would be late for the concert, he dressed hastily and declined all but Mrs Brook's excellent soup, much to that lady's displeasure. He was fastening his evening cape and rushing downstairs, when he heard Vince's key in the door.

'Can't talk now, lad.'

'I'll come with you to the cab stance.'

As they hurried along Sheridan Place and on to Minto Street, Faro gasped out the afternoon's events at the offices of Mr Franklin, ending with Alex Troup's revelations.

Vince halted in his tracks. 'So you were right. Eveline Shaw is Kellar's mistress. I can hardly believe it,' he added disgustedly. 'Poor Mabel. No wonder she was so desperately miserable, betrayed by her husband and her dearest friend and companion. I wonder why she didn't mention her name to Tiz.'

'I've no idea. Perhaps she didn't want to believe it.'

'That I can well imagine. She was the sort of person who would never believe evil of anyone. It makes my blood boil when I think of that dinner party. All that petting and cosseting – and all the time . . . How could she?'

'Yes, lad. I've been thinking along the same lines. This new evidence creates a bit of a poser. It doesn't take us anywhere, just creates a new puzzle. She never hinted anything to you? We know that she had her suspicions at Christmas.'

Vince shook his head. 'She did nothing but praise Eveline to me, what a wonderful friend. Her sister of the spirit, you know, the daughter she'd never had – all that sort of thing.'

'If she knew, then such an unworldly attitude, so saintly . . . '

Vince laughed softly. 'Oh, that was typical of her. Well, Stepfather, when are you going to arrest Kellar?'

'When we have a bit more evidence.'

'Haven't you got more than enough now?'

'Only circumstantial, I'm afraid. We still have to find the body.'

'It's too late, Stepfather. You must know that now from Mabel's letter. Kellar put the noose around his own neck. We have it in his own words when he bragged to her how easy it would be to dispose of a victim. The young vultures in the medical school will have reduced everything to indecipherable butcher's meat long since. Oh dear God, it's awful, awful,' Vince sobbed, leaning against the fence. 'She didn't deserve that.'

As Faro flagged down an approaching cab, Vince said bitterly, 'I hope you'll enjoy yourself. I'm glad it's not me. I'd hate to have to play the hypocrite and be nice to Eveline Shaw. She's as guilty as Kellar and I jolly well hope they both hang.'

Vince's words remained with Faro. He knew from earlier discussions about the disposal of bodies that even the head, unless required for demonstration purposes, could be dissolved in acid and nothing left but the skull. By the time he reached Regent Crescent he was so sunk in misery that he would have given a great deal to have had some other companion that evening.

But Mrs Shaw was awaiting him eagerly. Her happiness and excitement were so infectious that he resolved to firmly set aside for the evening the grim realisation that he might be in the company of a murderess. The lovely woman at his side had perhaps entreated and assisted her lover to get rid of the wife who stood in their way, but Faro soon found his self-confidence elated by stepping into the foyer of the Assembly Rooms escorting a lady whose youth and beauty turned every head in their direction.

Under the fur cloak Eveline Shaw wore a purple velvet gown, the fashionable bustle with its titillating glimpse of lilac lace petticoats showed off her tiny waist and exquisite figure to perfection.

Faro was charmed and flattered. Had she really blossomed out into half-mourning so splendidly on his account? He was heartily glad and relieved to have missed supper in order to change into evening dress, his top hat and opera cape and to take extra care over his own appearance.

Looking around in the interval, he was acutely conscious of the elegance of the concert-goers. Despite the fact that they and he wore the same correct attire for the occasion, there all likeness ended, for most were strangers to Faro's humble and often violent way of life. He lived daily with danger and sudden death. And here among the lawyers, judges, doctors, engineers, bankers and business men, was a stratum of Edinburgh life he rarely encountered socially and entered only from the professional viewpoint, often warrant in hand.

Some recognised him and moved away with a hasty backward glance, anxious not to be recognised. Faro smiled wryly. His contact with several of those concert-goers that evening was not one they would wish to acknowledge in public. And yet, listening to the buzz of talk around him, he realised that here they were all momentarily united in their love of music, discussing the programme and Hallé's powerful conducting of the orchestra in the Mendelssohn Hebrides Overture and his Third, 'Scottish', Symphony.

He found a corner seat and as Mrs Shaw gratefully sipped a glass of lemonade, he answered her question as to how it had all begun for him, this love of music.

'Many years ago, when I first came down from Orkney to join the police, I was sent here to arrest a Hungarian violinist who had been involved in a fraud case. Until that evening, all the music I had ever known was the Orkney fiddle, the fife, the drum, the clarsach. I had never heard so many instruments, wind, strings, all playing at the same time and making such heavenly sounds. Indeed, it was exactly what I expected of paradise. When I asked what they were playing, I was told it was Beethoven's Fifth Symphony. I was enthralled.'

'Did you catch your criminal?' Mrs Shaw asked gently.

'No. Not then. I was the one caught that night – caught by a passion for classical music that I have never lost.'

'Did you not have music round the piano at home?'

'Oh yes. But I had never appreciated that particular instrument until I heard it on the concert platform, in the hands of an expert.' He looked at her smiling. 'Divinely played, as it is when you play the Appassionata.'

'You are very kind.'

'Not at all. Just amazed that you are not up there yourself, on the concert platform. I feel certain that you did not reach such an amazingly high standard from taking piano lessons.'

She sighed. 'I was born into music. My parents were both musicians, the violin and the piano were their instruments. They had hopes that I too would become a professional and my childhood was dedicated to that high goal.'

Her face darkened and she shook her head sadly. 'Alas, they both died in a cholera epidemic and I was left on my own at sixteen. The aunt I was sent to in Caithness thought such ambitions far too grandiose for an orphan.' She stopped, frowning, as if reliving a particularly painful scene.

'A pity. Such a waste of talent,' said Faro.

'No, Inspector. It wasn't written for me, omitted from my chapter in the Book of Life, that's all. Anyway, it was very soon afterwards I met Barnaby's father . . . '

Ah, he thought, that careful and evasive phrasing gives nothing away. Before he could probe the subject further, the bell sounded marking the end of the interval.

Soon both he and Mrs Shaw were absorbed and captivated by Mme Neruda playing the Beethoven Violin Concerto in D. The thunderous applause and cries of 'Encore', were rewarded by a short virtuoso piece and at last the orchestra took their final bow.

The audience trooped out into the foyer to seek their carriages in the long waiting line extending down George Street and as Faro and Mrs Shaw stood under the brilliant lights from the candelabra, he was aware of admiring glances from young men and envious looks from their partners.

At his side, Mrs Shaw's eyes roamed constantly, and not in search of admiration, he realised as her hand tightened suddenly on his arm. Thinking she was about to bring someone to his attention, he turned and caught a glimpse of her expression. He was well aware of the miasma of fear after twenty years with the Edinburgh City Police. It was something so tangible, he could almost smell, see, and touch it.

Mrs Eveline Shaw was trembling and afraid.

A moment later, he saw the reason. The young man he had encountered at her front door was waiting on the steps. His eyes blazing in fury, left no doubt whom he was searching for. Mrs Shaw hesitated. He leaped up to her, hand upraised. The words he yelled were in Gaelic, but Faro was sufficiently familiar with the language to know that she was being cursed as a bitch and whore.

Outraged, Faro jumped forward, deflected the blow and was pushed aside.

'Keep out of this.'

Braver men than the one before him had lived to infinitely regret having laid hands on Detective Inspector Jeremy Faro. Now he raised his fists purposefully.

'Apologise to this lady, sir,' he threatened, 'or it will be the worse for you.'

Mrs Shaw dragged at his cape, adding her own entreaty. 'Keep out of this, Inspector. Please, for my sake.' And to the glowering young man, 'This is nothing to do with him. Please, Harry. He is just a friend of Mabel's. I beg you, please don't make a scene. Please.'

Suddenly the young man gazed down at her hand on his arm. Although he swept it aside, it had gentled him, like a wild stallion that feels the quieting caress of fond ownership.

He examined her face, looked deeply, beseechingly into her eyes, like one who searches for an answer.

'Harry, please listen, my dear,' she whispered.

But the momentary spell was broken and Harry threw off her hand again, this time violently. Turning, he quickly pushed his way through the crowd who had gathered silently, expecting a fight.

Ignoring stares and whispers, Faro tucked Mrs Shaw's trembling arm firmly into his own and led the way to the carriage that was awaiting them. She said nothing, crouched in the far corner like a hurt animal who wishes only to avoid all physical contact.

Once or twice on the journey back to Regent Crescent they stopped to give way to the traffic and, under the street lamps briefly illuminating the carriage, Faro saw her expression. Dazed and lost, that was how she now appeared, exactly as he remembered her from the Kellars' fateful dinner party.

She remained silent until her house was in sight. When the carriage stopped and Faro handed her down, she took his hand limply and said in a small exhausted voice, 'Thank you for this evening, Inspector. I am sorry, truly sorry, it had to end in such a way. Please accept my apologies.'

Running up the steps, she opened the door swiftly and hurried inside, as if afraid he might attempt to follow her.

But Faro was not prepared to depart without the explanation which he considered due to him. Afraid that Mrs Shaw was in danger from the violent young man, before taking his departure he required reassurances, and to offer his protection if necessary.

He raced up the steps. 'Wait. You have no need to apologise.'

She regarded him wide-eyed from behind the half-closed door. 'I find myself in a very difficult situation. Harry Shaw gets jealous . . . '

Shaw, thought Faro and said, 'He is related to you?'

Mrs Shaw seemed bewildered by the question. She shook her head, biting her lip.

'He is an acquaintance then?' Even as he said the words, Faro heard their echoing absurdity.

Mrs Shaw looked up into Faro's face sadly. 'Oh no, Inspector. He is more than that. Much more. He is my lover.'

Chapter Thirteen

Vince came down early next morning to join his step-father at breakfast, eager to hear about the concert with Mrs Shaw.

Faro described the scene outside the Assembly Rooms with Harry Shaw, the young man she claimed was her lover and whom he had met earlier that day, leaving her house in a temper.

Vince whistled. 'Now that is a surprise, Stepfather. Did Harry precede or succeed Captain Shaw? They must be related. Sounds as if she's got herself not only into a difficult situation but a right old pickle. And where does Dr Kellar fit into this new picture?'

Faro had much to occupy his thoughts as he walked down the Pleasance that morning and hurried towards the Central Office, where the mystery surrounding Mrs Shaw was beginning to unravel with considerably more speed than he had anticipated.

He was greeted by a triumphant and jubilant McQuinn. 'I've checked on the Caithness Regiment as you asked, sir. There isn't, and never has been, a Captain Shaw. He doesn't exist.'

So the late Captain Shaw who died fighting for Queen and country on the Indian frontier, leaving his grieving widow to bear him a posthumous child, had been a mere invention to appease convention. It raised some interesting speculations. Did this new piece of scandal, to be relished in due course by Edinburgh gossips, have any bearing on Mabel Kellar's murder?

But the most burning question of all remained unanswered. What part had Harry Shaw played in Mrs Kellar's disappearance? Kellar and Eveline Shaw had an alibi, they had spent that afternoon together. But was it, in fact, Harry Shaw who had been waiting for Mabel Kellar on the train where he had murdered her and helped dispose of her body?

A tap on the door and the constable on the desk duty gave him a note.

'Just found this, Inspector. It was handed in yesterday.'

Faro regarded him stony-faced. 'Yesterday! When yesterday, may I ask? There's no time stated.'

'It's a new young lad on the desk, sir. When you'd gone home, he probably thought it wasn't all that urgent.'

'He'll remember next time, that's for sure, if he hopes to stay in the police. Impress on your lad that this is an urgent missing persons case. McQuinn is my second and if he is unavailable, then I can be contacted at home.'

The note read: 'An errand lad brought a message from Dr Kellar's house. Mrs Flynn requires to see the Inspector only [the words were heavily underlined] as soon as possible.'

'Trouble, sir?' asked McQuinn, peering over his shoulder.

'You can come along and find out,' said Faro, handing him the note. 'This is something you could have dealt with.'

'But I wasn't— '

'Oh, never mind. Let's go.'

To the driver of the waiting police carriage he gave directions to the Kellar house where Ina opened the door, staring out at them with frightened eyes. 'It's to do with the mistress, sir.' She looked over her shoulder. 'I told you this was an evil house. I feel things.'

'What sort of things?'

'Presences,' she whispered.

She almost jumped into the air when the bell from the

housekeeper's room pealed through the hall. 'That's Mrs Flynn. She said I was to take you to her directly and not waste time gossiping.'

McQuinn made a grimace as Ina led the way downstairs. At the door of Mrs Flynn's gloomy apartments, Faro whispered, 'We'll talk to you later, Ina.'

'If you wish, sir.'

The housekeeper was lying on her bed. 'Ina?'

When the maid's scared face looked round the door, Mrs Flynn said, 'Here's the shopping list. Go as quick as you can. These things are needed for the master's supper.' And then to Faro, 'Excuse me not rising, Inspector. It's me veins. Bad they are just now.'

Faro decided the housekeeper was extremely unlucky in being so prone to indisposition. Every time he came he found her suffering from some new infliction. A sore throat, a bad leg and now she was back with the swathed jaw: presumably the toothache that had caused the initial disasters at the Kellar dinner table.

Following his gaze, she said. 'I'm nearly mad with that abscess again. Hardly closed my eyes last night.'

She certainly wouldn't last long in any employment at this rate, he thought, murmuring sympathy. 'But you really must do something about it, Mrs Flynn. The dentist can't be any worse than all this agony,' he said severely, and feeling no end of a hypocrite added encouragingly, 'It's all over in a minute, you know.'

The housekeeper shuddered. 'I'll have to think about it. I can't go on much longer like this.' Then, leaning forward, she whispered, 'I asked you to come because we found this in the chimney.'

From under the bed she withdrew a bundle.

'What is it?'

At first glance in the dim light, Faro thought he was seeing a bloodied, soot-streaked white seabird, which Mrs Flynn shook out to reveal a woman's petticoat. The bodice was heavily bloodstained.

'You say this was in the chimney, Mrs Flynn?'

'Yes, sir.'

'Tell me the whole story from the beginning, if you please.'

'It was just last week, sir, the chimney in the master's bedroom. He started complaining that it was smoking. Ina and I looked up but we couldn't see anything. It had been swept at Christmas so it couldn't be soot. He said to get a sweep. Well, that came down with the brushes.'

Spreading the garment on the table, even the bloodstains and the soot could not disguise that it was of fine-quality lawn and the lace was of exquisite workmanship.

'Do you recognise it?'

'Oh yes, Inspector. It belonged to the mistress. I ironed it the morning she left. She asked for it specially, one of her favourites.'

'You are absolutely sure this is the same garment she was wearing when she left?'

'Oh yes, sir. You see, as she was putting it on, she stepped on the lace and it tore. She asked me to sew it. If you'll hand it over – here, see – on the hem. I can recognise my own sewing,' she said proudly. 'I couldn't find the white cotton and as she was in a hurry I hoped she wouldn't notice that I used cream thread.'

Faro looked at the neat stitches. Cream against white, not particularly obvious, but the housekeeper's repair was further grim evidence that murder had been committed. The case against Dr Kellar was almost complete.

'If someone was trying to burn this garment, I don't understand why it was up the chimney?' At his side, McQuinn asked the logical question which had also been troubling Faro.

'I couldn't say, but it was rolled up in a tight ball,' said Mrs Flynn encouragingly. 'Inspector, may I ask you something?' When Faro nodded, she went on, 'The mistress – has she – is she – I mean, has she been done in by someone?'

'We don't know that, Mrs Flynn.'

'But, sir, what about the bloodstains in the coach? The fur cloak that the papers mentioned, and then there was the carving knife we missed from the kitchen. And now this . . . ' her voice grew shriller, as she pointed to the petticoat. 'What more do the police need to make an arrest, Inspector?'

'They need a body, Mrs Flynn.'

'A body, sir?'

'Yes, Mrs Flynn – a body.'

The housekeeper thought for a moment. 'Do you think the police will ever find her?'

'I expect so, if we're patient.'

Mrs Flynn shook her head. 'I don't think patience has much hope here. Not against him.'

'What do you mean?'

'Well, it's as plain as the nose on your face, Inspector. He spends his time cutting bodies up and, so I hear, giving bits to his students. Revolting, I call it, not even Christian burial, poor souls.'

As they were about to leave, taking the petticoat with them, Faro said, 'Perhaps we could have a word with the maid.'

'If she's back from the shops, yes. And she takes for ever. I'd better warn you, Inspector.' Mrs Flynn put a finger to the side of her head and twisted it significantly. 'She's not all there.'

'Simple, you mean?'

'That's right. Sees things. Ghosts and such rubbish. I've never felt or seen anything amiss in the house. I think she does it to make herself important.'

She struggled to rise from her bed. Putting her foot on the ground she gave an agonised gasp and Faro, bundling up the petticoat, said hurriedly, 'We'll see ourselves out.'

As they walked down the front steps, McQuinn said, 'Begging your pardon, Inspector, but this doesn't make sense to me. Everything points to Kellar having done his wife in, like the old housekeeper says. But if he put the petticoat up the chimney then he wouldn't have drawn attention to himself by complaining that it was smoking, would he? He could have burnt it, got rid of it somewhere else, couldn't he?'

'The only reason would be panic.'

'And from what I've seen and heard of that gentleman, he's a cool customer, sir.'

At that moment a hired carriage arrived, and the cool customer descended and paid his fare.

'We'll have the cab, sir. Wait a moment, if you please.'

Dr Kellar was looking decidedly flushed and ill. 'What do you want this time, Inspector?' he demanded irritably. 'Out with it quick, man. I've had to leave early. You must excuse me if I don't delay. Stomach cramps. There's a bit of drain fever about at Surgeons Hall – I think I must have caught a dose. Not helped of course by the vile cooking in my home these days. Well, what is it now?'

'We've solved the problem with your bedroom chimney.'

'Surely we didn't need to call in the police for that?'

'The sweep found this was causing the blockage,' said Faro pushing forward the petticoat.

'What's this? A woman's shift – what on earth?' Kellar sounded genuinely astonished.

'Do you recognise it?'

'No, should I?' When Faro didn't answer, Kellar said. 'Some damned servant girl larking around, I suppose.'

'I'm afraid not. We have reason to believe that it belongs to your wife.'

Kellar looked again and Faro thought he grew a shade paler. 'I've never seen it before.'

'Surely . . . ' Faro began.

'If you are asking me what my wife wore under her dresses, then I can only tell you I haven't the faintest idea.'

If they slept in separate rooms, thought Faro, then Dr Kellar was probably speaking the truth.

'So you wouldn't be prepared to identify it?' said Faro.

'No, I would not,' Kellar replied testily.

'You would agree then that the servants are better acquainted with your wife's undergarments.'

'Of course they are.'

'So what would you say if I told you that Mrs Flynn has identified it as belonging to Mrs Kellar, by a repair she did on the morning your wife disappeared?'

'I would only say, surely no one, not even you, would take the word of domestics against mine. Now I bid you good-day, gentlemen.'

Kellar hurried up the front steps and let himself into the house.

McQuinn looked at Faro as if expecting him to make some move to stop the doctor's hasty retreat. Faro shrugged and stepped into the waiting carriage.

'Waverley Station, if you please. I'm going back to Longniddry, McQuinn, see if there are any more developments. You stay here, try to be unobtrusive and talk to the maid when she gets back. Shouldn't be long,' he added, in response to McQuinn's sullen look.

When Faro stepped off the train at Longniddry, a railwayman standing at the far end of the platform waved frantically, as if he had been waiting for the Inspector.

'Thought I recognised you, sir. I'm Thomas. That was quick work, sir,' he added with a grin. 'I've just sent a message an hour ago, through one of your men working the line.'

'Another discovery?'

'No, just information, sir.'

'Good.'

Faro began to walk towards the barrier and Thomas put a hand on his arm and said, 'Do you think we could talk back here, Inspector? I don't particularly want Mr Andrews to see us together. Look, if we sit on the steps of the signal box there down the line.'

'I hope it won't take long,' said Faro, pulling up the collar of his coat against the bitter east wind.

'It's like this, sir. That afternoon when you asked the station master about ladies in fur cloaks. I was listening when he told you about the maids with their parcels helping their mistresses out of the station and into carriages and so forth. Well, I remembered something. I wasn't sure whether it was of any importance, but I've been thinking about it since . . . '

'Why didn't you speak up at the time?' demanded Faro crossly.

'Look, Inspector, when the station master, Mr Andrews, isn't on duty I'm in charge of collecting tickets. It's a punishable offence, a fine taken off my wages, if I let someone go without a ticket. So if I make a mistake, I keep quiet about it, see. It's happened a couple of times and I'm on my last warning. Next time it'll cost me my job. And I've got a wife and five wee ones . . . '

It was beginning to rain, rain that was turning into sleet.

'So,' said Faro trying not to sound urgent, 'what was it you remembered?'

'About ten minutes after the North Berwick train left that day, the one you were enquiring about, when all the passengers had gone and I was going to lock the gate, a maid came out of the waiting room. She was carrying a big parcel. I know all the lasses here but this one was a stranger and I said, '"You're lucky. Another minute and you'd have been locked in. Unless you're able to climb gates."

'She didn't say a word, searching for her ticket in her travelling bag. She was shivering and had no coat, just a shawl and it was snowing.'

'"Have you far to go, miss?" I asked her.

'"Just down the road."

'When she found the ticket I noticed it was all bloody. So were her fingers. "Cut yourself, miss?" I asked.

'She seemed put out. "Just a scratch. I was looking

for water to wash my hands and there is none on the train. None in the waiting room either."

'"Hold on, miss," I said, "and I'll get you water from the station master's room. We keep emergency bandages and things there in case of accidents."

'But when I came back two minutes later, she was scurrying off down the road, fast as her legs would carry her.'

'What was she dressed like?'

'Like, sir?' Thomas laughed. 'Like a maid, of course.'

'Young, old?'

'Difficult to say, sir. Fiftyish, I'd reckon. Hair tucked into a maid's cap.'

A picture was forming in Faro's mind. 'Spectacles?'

Thomas screwed up his face trying to think. 'Couldn't say as I noticed that, sir. But I don't think so.'

'Well then, was she a big woman? Stout, a bit clumsy-looking?'

'Oh, no, Inspector. A right skinny one. Tallish, thin as a post, this one. Nifty on her feet, I can tell you, the way she made off down the road. I guess she'll be from these parts, with one of the big houses.'

'What makes you think that?'

Thomas laughed. 'That's easy, sir. She had a first-class ticket.'

'First class? Surely that's unusual for a servant.'

'Not hereabouts, sir. The quality ladies do like to keep their maids by them in the same compartment, especially if the train's crowded. If she'd been travelling on her own, of course, she'd have been in third class, that's for sure.'

Faro had much to occupy his mind on the train back to Edinburgh.

The case against Kellar seemed now cut and dried. The fact that there was no Captain Shaw, allied to the revelations in Mabel's letter to her sister, confirmed Faro's own deduction about what had happened on that fateful train journey.

If he had been in any further need of convincing, the revelations of Thomas were proof positive that Mabel Kellar's body was beyond recovery. Kellar had condemned himself in his own words, most diabolically, by boasting to his wife how easy it would be for a police surgeon with access to a mortuary and dissecting room to dispose of an unwanted corpse.

Eveline Shaw had certainly provided Kellar with an alibi. But he needed an accomplice. Now, from the assistant ticket collector at Longniddry, it appeared they had found someone, in the guise of a maid, who had helped them get away with murder.

Chapter Fourteen

It was already dark when Faro at last walked up the steps to the Central Office. McQuinn was writing at the desk in his office. As his superior came in the sergeant threw down the pen.

'I was preparing a report for you, sir, before I went off duty.'

'Yes?'

'I stayed around at the back door of the Kellar house until the maid came back from the shops. The girl believes that she sees things, feels presences, but when I asked her to be more precise, all she did was shake her head and look like bursting into tears. It seems that Mrs Flynn has scared the living daylights out of the lass, that she'll lose her job. She's more anxious about that than her ghosts, I can tell you. Seems she has a dying sister and an invalid mother. Poor wee lass.'

He paused and gave Faro a speculative glance. 'I could try talking to her again, but it would have to be away from the house. She'd likely be easier without feeling that Mrs Flynn was watching her.'

Apart from his natural gallantry towards the female species at all times, Faro felt that McQuinn had little interest in carrying this particular professional duty into the realms of pleasure.

'Tell me, McQuinn, did you think the girl was – well, genuine?'

'Oh, I did, sir. No doubt about that. She's seen something in that house that scares her all right. Apparitions, well, I'm doubtful. I was wondering if it could be – let's say a corpse.'

'You mean the missing Mrs Kellar.'

'I was thinking along those lines.'

'I think you're wrong about that, McQuinn.' And Faro proceeded to tell McQuinn about the development at Longniddry.

McQuinn pushed back his helmet, scratched his head. 'Well, sir, that is a poser, isn't it? Looks like the murder was committed on the train, early on, soon after leaving Edinburgh, I'd say, by this accomplice posing as her maid. Then her body was got off the train, don't ask me how,' he added hastily, seeing Faro's expression.

'If our suppositions are correct, then it was collected by Kellar in his carriage at some pre-arranged place along the line.'

'It couldn't have been at a station, sir. Even if your accomplice was carrying off an allegedly sick and injured woman, how would they account for all that blood.'

'She could have been murdered by strangulation or by a stab wound in some vital place which would not have bled profusely. Kellar would know all about that. Her body was taken to the mortuary by Kellar, while the bogus maid got off at the next stop – Longniddry – carrying the evidence which was then disposed of down the railway embankment?'

McQuinn brightened. 'That fits, sir.'

Faro shook his head. 'No, it doesn't. We haven't taken into account that vital factor of happenstance. However, it's well worth careful consideration. You might be on to something and we can check the stations en route, see if anyone was carried off the train.'

As praise from his superior was notably rare, McQuinn looked pleased. 'What shall I do next, sir?'

'Try and see the maid again. Use your charm on her, McQuinn.'

'Right, sir,' said McQuinn and saluted smartly.

Ever since Longniddry, Faro had begun to see a flicker of light, appropriately enough, at the end of the tunnel. Light that obstinately reflected a very different pattern from the one he had envisaged up till now.

As was his custom, he had been marshalling his facts together and when he wearily let himself into 9 Sheridan Place, he was pleased to find Vince at home, anxious for an account of his day's activities.

Regarding the revelations from the Caithness Regiment, Vince said disgustedly, 'Imagine there being no Captain Shaw and all this time we've been falling over ourselves to console the distraught young widow. What a cheat!'

'Do you think Mrs Kellar knew the truth?'

'Certainly not. She would never suspect a friend of telling her such a downright lie. What else did you find out?'

Vince listened eagerly to Faro's account of the interview with Thomas. 'This is great progress, Stepfather. All you need now is to trace the maid. What a piece of luck.'

'There's one thing more, lad.' Faro was reluctant to tell his stepson about the bloodstained petticoat. As he expected Vince was exceedingly upset.

'How can you sit there, Stepfather, so calm and doing nothing about arresting Kellar. In the face of such damning evidence,' Vince added, thumping the table angrily.

'Vince, lad. Listen. Please, I beg you, don't get carried away by emotions.'

'Emotions!' Vince exploded. 'My most dear friend has been murdered by her husband, aided and abetted by her false friend. And you ask me not to get carried away!'

'Vince. Listen to me. I need some clear concise thinking on this, the kind that you have so often provided in the past. I beg of you to forget for the moment that you are personally concerned. Pretend that Mabel Kellar is just one other murder victim and help me. Help me, lad, when I most need you.' He paused. 'Will you do that, lad?'

Vince sat back in his chair and said stiffly, 'All right,

Stepfather. But do try not to make it difficult for me by talking about my emotions.'

'Very well. I apologise for my lack of tact. It won't happen again. Now, let's consider all these latest developments I've told you about. I've come to only one conclusion and that is, all is not what it seems.'

'What is that supposed to mean?' asked Vince irritably. 'Why, it's all plain as the nose on your face to anyone with half an eye.'

Faro suppressed a smile. This was no time to tease his stepson about ill-chosen metaphors. 'It's meant to be, but you have my assurances, it is not. I must ask you to believe in my judgement. We are not nearly there yet.'

'I should have thought that Mabel's petticoat in the chimney would be enough, without her cloak and the knife, to prove that someone in the house, and Kellar is the most likely since he has the motive, has got rid of her body and is desperately trying to get rid of the evidence.'

Faro nodded. 'That is certainly the obvious conclusion. But I want you to concentrate your thoughts in quite another direction.'

Vince continued to look distraught and angry and Faro went on, 'Kellar denies putting the petticoat up the chimney, or to recognise it as belonging to his wife.'

Vince laughed harshly. 'That doesn't surprise me. I imagine the housekeeper and the maid are more familiar with his wife's laundry than Kellar, seeing that they live quite separate lives.'

'Indeed, and Mrs Flynn recognised the garment immediately.'

'So there you are.'

'The snag about this particular piece of evidence is that Kellar was the one to complain about the smoking chimney in the first place, and insist on getting the sweep. I find it extraordinary that a guilty man would want to draw attention to himself in this way.

'Let's assume for the moment that Kellar is speaking

the truth.' Faro ignored Vince's snort of disbelief and went on, 'Who do we have left who could have done away with Mabel? Bear in mind that we are also looking for someone with a motive.'

'And for someone who could wield a carving knife with good effect, and dispose of a body,' said Vince. 'There can't be many in this particular *dramatis personae*.'

'I agree. And we're discounting a possible madman on the train.'

'It lets out Mrs Shaw who would be physically incapable of the deed, although she was doubtless the motive for the murder.'

'Yes. In her way, she is as guilty as Kellar,' said Faro sadly.

'What about Sir Hedley Marsh?'

'We've covered that ground before. Why should he murder his heiress? Besides, the Mad Bart is too well kenned a figure about Edinburgh to murder anyone on a train, even if he was fit enough physically to drag a body around.'

'I suppose the old man who does the garden is similarly innocent.'

'We had a routine check on him. He was in bed all that week with a bad attack of pleurisy,' said Faro.

'And the maid Ina can be dismissed on physical grounds. She's hardly built for that kind of murder. What about Mrs Flynn?'

'She's stout and undoubtedly strong, if she ever gets rid of her toothache and bad veins.'

Vince shook his head. 'Remember the motive, Stepfather. She and Ina loved Mabel. They would have done anything for her, just like everyone else fortunate enough to know her.'

Looking across at Faro, he said, 'If it wasn't Kellar, then our best bet is Harry Shaw. I'm sure the same thought has occurred to you. From what your Longniddry fellow told you, I got a distinct picture that the maid he described could have been a man.'

Faro gave a sudden start. 'Disguised, of course.'

'What was this man Shaw like?'

'Tallish, but lightly built.'

'There you are, Stepfather. That's your answer, just as you speculated. Shaw was persuaded, or coerced into helping them out. You have Mrs Shaw's word and the evidence of your own eyes that he is a violent man.' He paused and gave his stepfather an enquiring look. 'Are you taking this in? Surely you've seen the significance?'

Faro turned to face him slowly. 'It's beginning to dawn very clearly, lad. Yes, that light at the end of the tunnel is growing distinctly brighter, quite illuminating, in fact.'

Vince gave his stepfather an exasperated stare. 'Well, I'm glad to have been of some help.'

Faro smiled. 'Oh you have, lad. You have indeed.'

'Good. Let's take our supposition a bit further. Harry Shaw helps out, as you surmised with the evidence, perhaps with the murder on the train.'

Faro didn't answer. He drained his teacup of contents that had gone cold long since.

'And now with the obstacle to her marriage out of the way,' Vince continued, 'free to marry Melville Kellar at last, Mrs Shaw sends her inconvenient lover packing. But he has other ideas. If she is as diabolic as we are beginning to suspect, I rather think the next corpse might be Harry Shaw.'

Faro sprang from his seat. 'Get your greatcoat, Vince, we're going out.'

'Out? Where?'

'We're going to pay a couple of unexpected calls. First of all, to the Kellar house.'

'Stepfather, it's nearly nine o'clock.'

'So?'

'You can't call on Kellar uninvited at this hour.'

'He won't be at home. I'm rather banking on it as I noticed in the newspaper that he is giving a lecture to a learned society.'

'Then what— '

'Don't argue. We're wasting valuable time.'

'Have you seen the weather?' protested Vince. 'It's been snowing since six.'

But Faro was already in the hall, donning his overshoes.

'Are you going to arrest Kellar when he arrives home? Is that it, Stepfather? Have I convinced you? Do we have to look sharp, call unexpectedly, in case he makes a run for it?'

Faro shook his head. 'The purpose of this visit is for you to see Mabel's room. You've got what they call a corbie's eye for detail. You see, I can't get it out of my mind that there was something I missed, something I should have seen but didn't on that first visit.'

Fortunately the snow had ceased and the evening was brightly moonlit. Faro, however, was impervious to the beauties of the night and Vince found himself indulging in a monologue.

As the cab carried them towards the Grange, he saw that his stepfather was unusually silent, huddled into a corner of the carriage, chin sunk into his collar, asleep or deep in thought.

At last they turned into the drive of Kellar's house where Faro sprang to life again and told the driver to set them down. 'We'll walk the rest of the way. Wait for us here.'

As the house came into view, there were no cracks of light visible behind the closed shutters. 'We're too late. Presumably they're all abed,' said Vince hoping this would dissuade his stepfather from proceeding any further.

'Then we'll have to wake them up,' said Faro cheerfully.

The doorbell pealed, once, twice. Vince shuffled his feet uncomfortably. 'Kellar will be furious if he catches us, Stepfather.'

'Listen. Someone's coming.'

'Who is it?' A woman's muffled voice.

Vince gave him a startled glance and whispered, 'Mrs Flynn?'

'Mrs Flynn, it's Inspector Faro.'

'What do you want? Master's not at home.'

'It is you I want a word with, Mrs Flynn. Or Ina.'

'Ina's away home.' There was a short silence. 'We're all poorly. Seem to have been poisoned with something bad we ate.'

'Poison, eh,' whispered Faro. He gave Vince a significant glance, his face unusually excited in the bright moonlight. 'Mrs Flynn?'

There was no reply and he rapped sharply on the door. 'Mrs Flynn. Open the door, please.'

'I'm in my nightgown, Inspector.'

'This is police business, Mrs Flynn. We have to see Mrs Kellar's room again.'

'At this time of night! Who's with you, sir?'

'Dr Laurie, Mrs Kellar's friend.'

'Come back tomorrow.'

'No. Open the door. We'll be as quiet as mice and it won't take more than two minutes.'

His wheedling tone succeeded in getting the door unlocked. As they set foot in the hall, Mrs Flynn retreated modestly.

'I've turned up the gas for you. I'm away back to my bed.'

Faro led the way upstairs and opened the door of Mabel's bedroom. 'All right, Vince lad, now you tell me what it was that I missed, because I'm damned if I know.'

Vince followed Faro round the room. Soon the room was brilliantly illuminated under the glare of gaslight. 'It's all exactly as I remember it the last time I was here. Nothing odd, certainly nothing out of place.'

Faro was standing by the dressing table. He lifted the silver-backed brushes as he had on that first visit.

'Exactly,' he whispered to Vince. 'And that is precisely what was wrong. What has been nagging at me all this time. Look at these, lad. What do they say to you?'

Vince frowned. 'That they are exquisite, very valuable. Mabel was very proud of them.'

'Then, tell me, why did she leave them behind?'

Vince watching his stepfather's reflection in the mirror, looked puzzled. 'I have no idea. Mabel was very proud of her hair; brushing it was a bit of a ritual with her and that's why she mourned the loss of a personal maid.'

'So you would agree that these are intimate articles that no woman would be without on her travels.'

'Certainly Mabel wouldn't.'

And Faro knew he had the answer to what nagged him since that first visit.

'Don't you see what this means, Vince, lad? There was something far more sinister behind Mabel Kellar's departure than a mere domestic tiff with her husband.'

Vince continued to look puzzled and Faro went on solemnly, 'What you are seeing now is the very first clue.'

'Clue, Stepfather. I don't understand.'

'Yes, you do, lad. Think. The presence of those hair brushes when they should logically have been absent tells us something vital about this whole case.'

Leaving Vince still staring blankly at the silver brushes, Faro led the way downstairs. Once Vince stumbled and cursed.

In the hall, Faro paused. 'We'll have a word with Mrs Flynn before we go.'

'If Kellar arrives and finds us roaming about his house at the dead of night, there'll be hell to pay,' warned Vince.

'This won't take a moment.'

But they were out of luck. Faro went downstairs, tapped on the door of Mrs Flynn's room from which loud snores issued forth. He called her name several times, but the snoring seemed to have intensified. Turning the handle, he found the door firmly locked.

'What did you expect, Stepfather? With a madman still

at large, and a maid who sees things, she's not taking any chances. And neither should we,' he added with a shudder. 'Do let's go. This house is cold as a tomb and it's beginning to give me the creeps.'

Vince sighed with relief when he saw the cab driver's lights along the drive. 'Home again, Stepfather. I'll be glad of a dram, I can tell you.'

'Not quite yet, lad. In a wee while.' And, leaning forward, Faro gave Mrs Shaw's address.

Vince looked aghast. 'You can't be serious, Stepfather, calling on her at this hour.'

'The later the better. With luck we might also find Harry Shaw there. An unexpected pleasure you have in store, lad,' he added, ignoring Vince's grumbles as they boarded the carriage and headed towards Regent Crescent.

Chapter Fifteen

Edinburgh asleep under its heavy blanket of snow presented a scene of enchantment and delight for those inclined to romance. At this hour there were few people about to enjoy this spectacular backdrop and Faro's entreaty to his stepson to admire such unexpected beauty met with a somewhat disgruntled response.

'All in bed and missing it, are they? I wish I was too, or I wish that my feet were warm. I'm frozen.'

Faro suppressed a smile at Vince's return to the spoilt petulant child of former years. There was nothing to be done with him in this mood, his stepfather knew from experience, and instead stared out of the window, sighing deeply as if he could breathe in the moonbeams.

When at last they reached Regent Crescent, the fanlight showed illumination and their summons was answered with alacrity by Mrs Shaw. In a dressing gown with her hair unbound she presented a captivating sight. She did not seem perturbed by their late arrival and greeted them without surprise.

'As if gentlemen arriving on her doorstep at nearly eleven o'clock was a perfectly normal occurrence,' Vince murmured later in shocked tones. The significant look he gave his stepfather indicated that Mrs Shaw had slipped from the pedestal of unsullied virtue into the realms of scarlet womanhood.

'Do come in,' she said cutting short Faro's apologies for the lateness of the hour. 'How nice to see you again, Vince. Barnaby is teething and refuses to settle. I have had him up and down since teatime.' Ushering them into the drawing-room as she spoke, she stirred the embers of the fire into a welcome blaze. 'Now what can I do for you?'

Faro and Vince exchanged uncomfortable glances staring at the baby lying on the sofa, attacking a teething ring with cannibalistic venom. It wasn't going to be easy.

Mrs Shaw went over and, after kissing Barnaby, smiled at them. 'Let me guess the purpose of your visit. I suppose it's about the late Captain Shaw.'

Faro nodded, cleared his throat a little, while Vince shuffled his feet and tried to look unobtrusive. 'That is so.'

Again she smiled, sadly this time. 'I realised that the police enquiries would be very thorough if you were in charge, Inspector. It was bound to come out sooner or later that I did not in fact have a husband and have never had one.'

Barnaby uttered a yell of protest and she swept him up into her arms, laid one scarlet cheek against her cool one.

'Perhaps you would give us the whole story. That would help enormously and save a great deal of time.'

'There is not much to tell. I met Harry Shaw when I went to live in Caithness after my parents died. Harry asked me to marry him but his taste for adventure decided me against it. He wished to go to America and I wished to remain in Scotland. There seemed to be no solution. We quarrelled and I sent him away. A few weeks later Dr Kellar came on a shooting holiday and was very attentive.'

She coloured slightly at the memory. 'I am very ashamed of what happened next. I had discovered that I was carrying Harry's child. I was desperate. Harry had gone out of my life for ever. My relatives would show me the door when they found out. There was only one solution left and however despicable it must sound to you, I had to find a father for my baby.

'I need not elaborate on the rest of the story, Dr Kellar's

infatuation and our subsequent association. I knew he was married but I followed him to Edinburgh and allowed him to set me up in this house, believing, God forgive me, that Barnaby was his child.'

She smiled sadly. 'His eagerness to do so astounded me. He never questioned or doubted my word. And he loved Barnaby from the first moment he set eyes on him, so proud to be a father at last.'

'Did he say he would marry you, if he were free?'

'Of course, but we both knew that was quite impossible and a scandal would have ruined him, destroyed his career, his hopes for the future. For me there was another factor: as I got to know Mabel and she was eager to befriend me as a young widow, I could not bear to have her hurt.'

She paused, looking at them from one to the other. 'But perhaps my strongest reason of all was that, despite our relationship, I in no way responded to Melville's infatuation. I knew how foolish I had been to reject Harry. I had given my heart. I still loved him and would do so always, even if I never saw him in this world again.'

She let the words sink in before continuing. 'I was the happiest woman in the world the day that Harry Shaw walked into this house, told me he still loved me and met his son for the first time.' Her eyes filled with tears. 'Oh, what a joyous meeting that was. The answer to a miracle indeed.'

She spread her hands wide in a gesture of hopelessness. 'Until I remembered Melville Kellar and his demands upon my life. What was I to do? I decided there must be no more secrets between Harry and myself and, I must say, he took it all remarkably calmly. He said he forgave me, but that I must write to Kellar and tell him the true facts. I'm afraid I tried several times, but always my courage failed me. My rapturous joy over Harry's return was every day slipping further into the realms of nightmare as we began to quarrel once again, for he thought my cowardice was lack of love for him.'

Barnaby began to whimper again as if in tune to his mother's sadness and she took him into her arms.

'It would be best, don't you see,' said Faro gently, 'if you were to write that letter.'

She looked up. 'But I have just done so. Harry posted it on the way to the station. I thought that was why you were here.'

'Where is Mr Shaw?' asked Faro.

'On his way to Yorkshire, for an interview with a firm of architects.'

'Then you are here alone?'

Mrs Shaw smiled at Faro's tone of alarm. 'I am used to being alone. I have my maid.'

'And yet you open the door to callers at this late hour?'

'I never gave it a second thought.'

'Then I urge you to do so.'

Her amused expression turned into a frown. 'Are you trying to warn me, Inspector. Am I in danger? I assure you I have no enemies.'

'All of us have enemies, whatever face they choose to wear.'

'You think Melville, when he finds out about Harry?' Her eyes widened in shocked surprise.

'I think nothing. I merely warn you to take extra care who you open your door to, especially at night.'

As they took their leave, bowing over her hand, Faro again urged her to be vigilant.

In the cab carrying them homeward at last, Vince mulled over the interview with Mrs Shaw. 'I still think of her as that.'

'And so she is under the Scottish law, Harry Shaw's wife "by habit and repute".'

'Of course. Well, this demolishes all our theories about the three of them conspiring to get rid of Mabel. I'm pleased about that.' He sighed. 'And if there were any reasons for joy in this miserable business I'm delighted that Melville Kellar has got his deserts and that Eveline Shaw's child isn't his after all.'

'It has a happier ending than perhaps she deserved.'

'The oldest trick in the world, Stepfather. Women have played that particular game since time began. And I have nothing but contempt for them. It is utterly vile, the ultimate unforgivable deception.'

'We must not let Mrs Shaw's revelations divert us from the main issue, lad.'

'I'm not forgetting, Stepfather. But you seemed remarkably worried, warning her about enemies and so forth, when she made it plain that she has none.'

'Oh yes, lad. She has one at least. I just hope to God that her letter arrived in time to avert yet another calamity and save her becoming the next victim.'

'Kellar, eh? I'd have liked to have been a fly on the wall when he read her letter of rejection,' said Vince with some relish. 'He must have been devastated, don't you agree?'

'I'm too tired to think straight any more, lad. What we both need is a dram and a good night's sleep. Everything will seem a lot clearer in the morning.'

But Faro, for once, was wrong.

He and Vince were indulging themselves with breakfast later than usual when the doorbell pealed shrilly through the house. They heard Mrs Brook come up from the kitchen, and by the time Faro had sprung from the table, Sergeant McQuinn was standing in the hall.

An unlikely figure to launch a thunderbolt set to reduce all Faro's new-found theories, his enlightened deductions to naught, he said, 'You're to come at once, sir, and bring the doctor along too. Kellar has shot himself.'

In the police carriage, McQuinn told them what had happened. He had been on his way to talk to the maid Ina before going on duty, when who should come along the drive, staggering through the snow but Kellar himself.

'Came out of the front gate, like a drunk man, wearing

nothing but his nightshirt. Then I saw the blood on the snow, dripping from his head it was. And when I went to help him, I could smell the gun smoke on him. I blew my whistle, got him into a passing cab and rustled up a couple of lads on the beat to take him across to the Royal Infirmary, quick as you like.'

He stopped. 'I was in a bit of a quandary, sir. I thought I'd best get back to the scene of the crime, so to speak.'

'You did quite right.'

McQuinn nodded. 'Went down that drive sharp as I could and there was Mrs Flynn standing at the door. Crying and wringing her hands. I could see she was in a terrible state.

'She'd been making breakfast when she heard a loud bang, that's how she described the pistol shot, coming from the master's bedroom. She went up to see what was wrong and there he was lying across the bed, with a bullet wound in his head, blood everywhere. At first she thought he was dead, then he groaned and moved. She realised he had tried to commit suicide. Here's the evidence, sir.'

He handed Faro a bloodstained note. Written in shaky capitals were the words: 'Goodbye, I killed her.'

'And here's the pistol I collected. There was this letter too, open on the bedside table. As it might be evidence, I took the liberty . . . '

The letter was from Mrs Shaw telling Kellar that she had deceived him, that Harry Shaw, who was Barnaby's father, had returned to Edinburgh and she was resolved to marry him.

'Did you read this, McQuinn?'

'Just a glance, sir. Evidence enough to prove that he got such a shock that his mind was temporarily unhinged. Mind you, he didn't strike me as the kind who would take his own life over any woman. Come ten a penny to a man like him.'

'Keep the contents to yourself, McQuinn, if you please.'

'Naturally, sir,' McQuinn sounded indignant. 'I suppose you'll need the servants to testify.'

Faro nodded rather absently, and the Sergeant gave him a curious look. The Inspector seemed almost as shocked as the housekeeper at the Grange had been.

'Mrs Flynn had a terrible fright. She told me when she saw he was still breathing, she rushed downstairs to get water to bathe his head – rushing around like a decapitated hen, I shouldn't wonder.' He grinned. 'Nothing as exciting as this had ever happened to her before. But when she got back to the bedroom, he had gone. Disappeared.'

As they boarded the carriage, Vince heard Faro giving McQuinn instructions about a locked cupboard he might expect to find. But no further explanation was offered to his bewildered stepson as they hurtled along towards the hospital as fast as the appalling condition of the snowy roads would allow.

Dr Kellar was occupying a private ward and, at first glance, Faro thought they had come too late. Kellar, with his head heavily bandaged, seemed to have a precarious grip on life.

'Looks pretty bad, doesn't he?'

Vince nodded. 'Can't really tell, until the doctors have had a chance to see how much damage was done by the bullet. I think I'll stay. This might take a little time.'

'Yes, yes, lad. I'll leave you to it. I'd better get back to the Grange and talk to Mrs Flynn and Ina.'

Vince looked at him frowning, seemed about to say something, then changed his mind and shook his head.

'What is it, lad?'

'Nothing, Stepfather. Just a thought. It'll keep.' And he turned his attention back to the doctors who were hurrying down the corridor to attend the injured man.

As the police carriage made its way through the melting snow taking Faro back towards the Grange, a sudden burst of sunshine, bringing with it unseasonal warmth, had set the birds singing an anthem to spring in the skeletal trees. Faro shook his head. This time of hope, this suggestion of springtime was all wrong for sudden death.

McQuinn was waiting for him and when they ran up the steps to the front door it was opened a couple of inches by a scared-looking Ina.

At the sight of the Inspector, she became quite voluble, sobbing out all about the master and the pistol shot and how poor Mrs Flynn had been frightened out of her wits.

'Easy, lass. Easy now,' said McQuinn gently. 'No one's going to harm you. We're here to help you.'

Faro noted that once again the handsome young sergeant's charm proved effective and the girl smiled at him gratefully through her tears as if she had been offered manna from heaven.

'We're here to see Mrs Flynn. Downstairs, is she?'

Ina shook her head. 'No, sir. She's gone to the Infirmary. To see how the master is. So upset she was. Terrible bad fright she got. Thinking he was dead, and then him walking away like that. Said it was enough to give anyone a heart attack.'

'Ina showed me the cupboard,' McQuinn interrupted, removing a travelling bag from under the hall table. 'That's all there was. It isn't locked.'

Faro glanced inside, nodded with some satisfaction and said. 'Come along, McQuinn. Back to the infirmary.'

Ina seemed reluctant to lose them. She followed them down the steps to the waiting carriage.

'You take care of things, Ina. You're in charge until we get back,' said McQuinn, making her feel important.

'But— '

'You'll be all right. I'm leaving a couple of constables to look after you,' he added, making her feel safe too.

As they got into the carriage, she giggled slightly hysterically. 'Poor Mrs Flynn. That fright didn't do her any good, I can tell you. I've always thought of her as such a big strong woman, but when I saw her hurrying down the drive, she didn't seem like herself at all. Dazed and scared-like. Isn't that amazing?'

Faro stared at her and slammed the door. 'Hurry, for God's sake. Fast as you can,' he told the driver.

The short journey to the Infirmary seemed endless and Faro drummed his fingers on the window-ledge, cursing the delays. What if they were already too late?

Reaching their destination, he leaped up the stairs to the ward, telling McQuinn to wait in the corridor.

'We may need you,' he added grimly. And to the nurse who approached. 'Has anyone been in to see Dr Kellar?'

'He is far too ill to receive visitors, Inspector,' was the shocked reply.

'That wasn't my question, Sister.'

'A Mrs Findlay-Cupar called a few moments ago.'

'Mrs Findlay-Cupar? Are you sure?'

'Yes, his sister-in-law.'

'Where is she now?'

'I sent her away, Inspector.'

'You sent her away?'

'Of course. My instructions are to admit no one. And that includes members of the family.'

In the ward, Faro was relieved to see Vince sitting at Kellar's bedside taking his pulse.

'Still alive, thank God.'

'I think he has a good chance,' said Vince cheerfully, 'Lucky for him, the bullet didn't strike any vital part. It grazed off the side of his head. He must have moved at the last moment. He's got a head as thick as a stone wall. Pity he'll only survive for the hangman's rope.'

The man on the bed groaned, opened his eyes, struggled to sit up and was restrained by Vince.

'Where am I?'

'The Infirmary, sir.'

Kellar blinked furiously. 'Thank God. Thank God, I can see. My head feels terrible. Am I going to die?'

It was a difficult question to answer in all honesty. Faro thought that 'Not just for the moment' would be inappropriate and rather unfeeling for the man's present condition.

'You're not seriously hurt, sir,' said Vince. 'The bullet deflected.'

'Ah, it's you, is it, Laurie, I hope you're remembering all I've taught you,' he said dazedly.

'Yes, sir.'

There was a short pause and then Kellar turned his head slowly towards them. 'All this is really happening. It isn't just a bad dream, is it?'

'No, sir. Unfortunately not.'

Kellar smiled wanly. 'I can see,' he repeated. 'I'm not blind or imagining things. So it was her.'

'Her? Who, sir?'

'Flynn.'

'When did you see her, sir?'

'She tried to kill me.'

'Mrs Flynn – the housekeeper – she tried to kill you?' said Vince and, looking across at Faro, whispered, 'His mind's wandering. He's having hallucinations.'

Kellar gave another groan and sank back on to the pillows. 'I'm telling you. She tried to kill me.'

Chapter Sixteen

Further questions were cut short by the arrival of the senior doctors. Faro was hustled into the tiny waiting-room by the grim-faced nurse, with Vince protesting furiously, 'How dare they treat me like a first-year medical student.'

Allowing his injured pride to be calmed down by his stepfather at last, he said, 'Kellar's mind must have been deranged. Or was it an attack of conscience?'

'An attack certainly,' said Faro, 'and by something much more substantial than conscience.'

'You mean, someone tried to kill him and make it look like suicide?'

'Exactly.'

'But the note— '

'I think we can dismiss the suicide note. The handwriting is not even a clever forgery.' Faro looked at the shaky capital letters. 'Look at the bloodstains. A man does not decide to shoot himself and write the note afterwards, although I imagine we are expected to make that account for the illegibility.'

'You're right, Stepfather. Kellar was no bungler. He was a highly efficient man and if he had been intending to kill himself it would have been done very tidily indeed.'

'Aren't you forgetting Mrs Shaw's letter of rejection?'

'A blow to his pride, but hardly enough to make him take his own life. Unless he realised that he had murdered Mabel for nothing. And talking of bloodstains, I'm working on the fur cloak. Using Dr Landois's experimental technique, I took a spot of blood from my finger and from Mrs Brook's. She was most impressed. However when I raided her pantry for raw beef, she was quite shocked, I can tell you. I've sent it off to Landois, although I'm not too hopeful of anything conclusive. As I told you, his experiments are in the early stages.'

'I think we'll hear that the bloodstains aren't human and that the blood doesn't correspond with either yours or Mrs Brook's. They most probably came from an ox heart or liver from the Kellar kitchen.'

'I don't understand. Why on earth should anyone counterfeit bloodstains?'

'The answer is easy. Dr Kellar was to be accused of his wife's murder.'

'Are you trying to tell me that there were to be two murders. The doctor and his wife?'

'No, I don't mean that at all. Kellar was always the intended victim, not Mabel. That was how it was planned, very carefully, right from the beginning.'

Ignoring his stepson's exclamation of disbelief, Faro continued, 'Right in fact from that fateful dinner party. That was all part of the plan too and the events of that evening are of vital importance. Nothing that happened that evening is too trivial to overlook, for it was all set out for us, like a play on a stage, a plot that had been worked out to the very last detail— '

'But I don't see how— ' Vince interrupted.

'We were all invited for a definite purpose, with our parts to play. We were to be witnesses of certain happenings. I was puzzled, I have to admit. My first thought was that I was there as a parent to give his approval and blessing on a piece of matchmaking between his stepson and a pretty widow— '

Faro cut short Vince's protest. 'Hear me out, please. My role was as audience to a curtain raiser on a very clever crime, the death of Dr Melville Kellar.'

'And Mabel?'

Faro smiled. 'You're going too fast, lad. Let us return to our arrival at the Kellar house. I want you to remember, if you can, every detail of our reception from the moment we walked up the drive.'

'The door was opened by the housekeeper— '

'Too fast. We rang the bell— '

'We rang the bell,' said Vince impatiently. 'And we had rather a long wait— '

'Ah, yes. Why?' he added sharply.

Vince shrugged. 'Lack of servants.'

'Why?'

'Mrs Kellar had given the maid Ina the weekend off and she and Mrs Flynn were cooking dinner. They were both in the kitchen and I presume hadn't heard us ring the bell.'

'Can you remember which of them opened the door?'

'Mabel – no, Mrs Flynn.'

'Did you notice anything about her?'

Vince thought. 'She was very hot and flustered, dusting flour from her hands.'

'Good. Floury hands which indicated that she was indeed in the process of making pastry. Tell me, what were your impressions of Mrs Flynn?'

Again Vince shrugged. 'Mrs Flynn? Why, none at all. I doubt very much whether I'd know her again if I met her.'

'You can do better than that, lad, after all I've taught you. What did she look like?'

Vince shrugged. 'I don't know. Just like any other maid. I didn't pay particular attention to her appearance.'

'Ah!'

Vince stared at him. 'It's true. She made absolutely no impression. A middle-aged domestic. Let me think. Was her hair grey?'

'What could be seen under her cap – yes. Did you notice anything about her eyes, for instance?'

'You surely don't expect me to remember the colour

of her eyes, Stepfather,' Vince protested. 'I'm bad at that, even for my nearest and dearest. Wait a moment, was she wearing spectacles?' He looked at Faro for affirmation.

'Good. Do you remember anything odd about her face?'

'Odd? Let me think. Oh yes, of course, she was all muffled up, swollen with toothache.'

Faro smiled. 'Good. You're more observant than you thought. You have described Mrs Flynn more or less exactly.'

'That's a relief,' said Vince sarcastically, thinking that this dinner party step by step was going to be almost as long and boring to recall as it had been in reality. 'So we enter the house. We go upstairs and are ushered into the drawing-room, introduced to Mrs Shaw.'

'Not so fast, lad. We are in the hall. Mrs Flynn apologises for the delay due to the lack of servants. Then Dr Kellar appears— '

'On the landing outside the drawing-room and rages at the housekeeper for keeping us waiting. He tells her to summon her mistress immediately.'

'Splendid. So where was our hostess, anyway, and why wasn't she there to greet her guests?'

'That's easy. She was in the kitchen. Mrs Flynn said so and Mabel confirmed that later.'

'Very well. We have Mrs Flynn answering the door and Mrs Kellar in the kitchen, helping the stricken housekeeper with some very indifferent cooking, out of the kindness of her heart, as there was no other servant in the house that night. In fact, we realised she had been hard at work until the last minute before dressing, for when she appeared at the dinner table there was still distressing evidence of pastry making on her hands and nails.' He paused to let this information sink in.

'Hardly an auspicious beginning, was it? Chaos in the kitchen, a housekeeper with raging toothache and no other servant?'

Faro smiled and wagged an admonishing finger. 'Ah yes, but a most auspicious overture for a planned murder. Keep that information by you, Vince. What could be better for our murderer's purpose than comings and goings of a very furtive nature without witnesses?'

Vince looked slightly dazed.

'We went upstairs and the drawing-room was occupied by Dr Kellar and Mrs Shaw, presenting the appearance of polite strangers who have no interest whatever in each other.'

'Yes, it was odd, when you think about it, that Kellar made no attempt to introduce us. Rather rude, I thought.'

'Well, we have the answer to that part of the mystery. The assembled company were meant to see antipathy between Mrs Shaw and Dr Kellar in the little charade put on for our benefit.'

'Because they were lovers?'

'Had been lovers, Vince. But Kellar wasn't aware then that Mrs Shaw planned to reject him.'

'That accounts, I suppose, for her own rather distraught manner.'

'Indeed it does. She was wondering how to break the news and, more important, what his reaction would be. However, they weren't the only ones with a charade to present that evening. You were sitting next to Mrs Shaw and Mabel.'

Vince gave him an impish look. 'And the only time I saw a spark of animation was when she was chatting to you or playing the piano.'

'Ah, the entertainment. We mustn't forget that. Mrs Shaw's excellent playing and Mrs Kellar's long monologue.'

'I'd heard it before. I thought she was particularly good at all those changes of voice.'

'An excellent mimic.'

Vince looked hard at him. 'I didn't think you shared my enthusiasm. I'm afraid you were looking very bored and so was Mrs Shaw who seemed as embarrassed by her friend's performance as she was by her fulsome affection. We know why, now.'

'Bad enough being in the same room with Kellar, dining at the same table with his wife, the dearest friend she had also betrayed. But let us leave Mrs Shaw now.'

'Poor Mabel,' said Vince. 'I keep thinking how dreadful the realisation must have been for her, how shattering. If she'd had the least idea, I'm sure she would never have given Mrs Shaw houseroom.'

'I think she knew at Christmas.'

'Then when she wrote to her sister, why didn't she say so in as many words?'

'Ah, that letter, Vince. Revealing all, which was precisely what it was meant to do.'

Vince frowned. 'But even the most forgiving of women . . . Her behaviour doesn't make sense.'

'Oh yes, it does. Very good sense indeed. Think of the contents of that letter, Vince, and what they implied.'

'I am thinking.'

'Let's return to our charade of a dinner party. What else could Mabel Kellar do in the circumstances? Kellar has told her that Mrs Shaw is his mistress, she has borne him a child and he has set her up in a house in the New Town. What was to be gained by admitting that she knew? Divorce, or a scandal, would not bring her erring husband back to her. By ruining his chance of a knighthood, she also had a lot to lose, her social standing in society, for instance.'

'True enough, Stepfather. Many women endure such an existence. Even knowing that their husbands, respectable men holding high positions in society, are leading double lives with a mistress and often an illegitimate child, they are in a cleft stick. A respectable marriage bestows on a wife a desirable place in society and if her husband falls, then she falls with him.

'What must have made it worse, unbearable for Mabel,

was the knowledge that she had been deliberately deprived of finding solace in the comfort of motherhood, and by her own husband.'

'Exactly,' said Faro triumphantly. 'So now you tell me, who had the best motive for murder that evening?'

'Mabel, of course,' laughed Vince. 'If she'd been the murdering kind she'd have stuck the carving knife in Kellar. I've always said that.'

'So you have, so you have.'

But ignoring his stepfather's gratified expression, Vince continued, 'Ironic, isn't it. Poor Mabel. No wonder they wanted to get rid of her. Her continued devotion to them both must have been a source of embarrassment. Mabel, so gentle and loving. But murder, such a terrible step to take.'

'To many desperate people, murder is the last resort and only terrible if they are found out. Within the police we are fully aware that husbands constantly murder wives, and t'other way round in our community, mostly for gain of some kind. Although our suspicions are aroused, we can rarely raise enough evidence to prove that a crime has been committed.'

Vince nodded in agreement. 'I know from conversations I've had with other doctors that they often had strong suspicions that poison has been administered. The discreet and effective way of certain death, although alas, slow and often very painful, it can be diagnosed as food poisoning, or drain fever. But doctors are often hesitant and dare not bring a case against some respectable citizen, for fear of putting their own reputations into jeopardy.'

'Aye, and many a timorous spouse ill-treated by husband or wife would commit murder – they do so in their hearts every passing hour – if they knew they could get away with it. The one deterrent is the indisputable evidence in the shape of a dead body, that cannot be conveniently spirited away.'

'Not in Kellar's case. Who had better facilities for

disposing of a corpse than Melville Kellar? He had a hundred unknowing accessories all ready and willing to help him dispose of the body beneath eager dissecting scalpels at Surgeons Hall. No body, no murder. Dear God, it must have seemed so easy, so foolproof.'

'Ah now, Vince, I see you're thinking along the same lines as the murderer. So let's leave the dinner party now and consider what happened next morning. You visited Mrs Kellar and found her packing in readiness for a short visit to her sister at North Berwick.'

Vince nodded. 'Her behaviour was certainly agitated but not more so than might be expected in a wife who had decided to run away from her husband and had a train to catch,' he added wryly.

'And after you left, she was seen by Mrs Flynn leaving the house, having had an altercation with Dr Kellar who was to set her down at the railway station.'

'We know she never reached North Berwick,' said Vince.

'And the Doctor didn't hear for a week, until a letter from Mrs Findlay-Cupar was found on her desk. This apparently had not been handed to Kellar by Mrs Flynn. Quite normal behaviour in the circumstances. Mrs Flynn said she didn't recognise the writing and it was addressed to the mistress personally.'

Faro smiled at Vince. 'That was very convenient. All communication between housekeeper and master was limited to notes left on the hall table regarding menus. Our murderer made very good use of the fact that Dr Kellar hated servants and avoided them at all times,' he added thoughtfully.

'And then the clues to Mrs Kellar's murder began to appear. Her bloodstained fur cloak and the carving knife, which was reported missing to me by the maid Ina. This evidence would have appeared much sooner, of course, had it not been for the weather and the fact that they lay undetected under a heavy snowfall for longer than was intended.'

Vince thought for a moment. 'But she couldn't have been murdered on the train. There would have been far too much blood, commotion. Trains at that time are full of folk going home for dinner. No, no. That wouldn't work at all.'

'What is your theory then?'

'You know that perfectly well, Stepfather. It's the only logical solution. Kellar never put her on the train at all. He offered to drive her to her sister's, murdered her in the carriage— '

'Hence the bloodstained upholstery,' Faro interrupted, 'Reported to me by Ina, via Mrs Flynn, but conveniently obliterated – if it ever existed – before I arrived. Go on, so what happened to the body?'

'He carried her under cover of darkness to the mortuary, cut her into more convenient pieces for distribution among his students,' Vince added with a shudder.

'You're quite wrong there. Think again, Vince. Why should Kellar take the carving knife with him and murder his wife in his own carriage. Why should he use a knife at all, when he could have strangled her without difficulty and then disposed of her body in the dissecting room? The bloodstained cloak and knife were accessories to murder that we were meant to find, so was Mabel's bloodstained petticoat stuffed up the bedroom chimney. Think about that, Vince.'

'Presumably he put it there hoping it would burn.'

'And then he got very angry and complained to the servants when it smouldered and filled the room with smoke. Is that logical behaviour? The chimneys had been swept recently, the sweep was re-called and discovered the petticoat, exactly as he was meant to. Why should Kellar, knowing what was in the chimney and in his bedroom because he had put it there, deliberately bring attention to his own guilt?'

'The behaviour of a very scared man.'

'Or the deliberate action of a very clever murderer.'

Vince frowned. 'I agree. There is something wrong here. It doesn't add up to what we know of Kellar.'

'Correct. The answer is that he was speaking the truth. He hadn't the least idea of what was causing his chimney to smoke. As you've pointed out, there are too many inconsistencies here and I think, once again, we have to go back to that train journey.'

'That's it,' said Vince triumphantly. 'The maid with the parcel at Longniddry. Of course.'

Faro pointed to the travelling bag. 'There is the final clue, lad, to what happened. The secret of the locked cupboard, you might call it, in Mrs Flynn's kitchen.

'I don't know what you're talking about, Stepfather, but I'm suitably intrigued, although I doubt whether Mrs Flynn will be pleased.'

'You needn't concern yourself any further about Mrs Flynn.'

'But— '

'You have my assurances of one thing. We will never see Mrs Flynn again.'

'You mean – that she has been murdered too?' said Vince in horrified tones.

They were interrupted by a tap on the door and McQuinn looked in.

'The doctors have left now.'

'Very well. Come along, Vince.'

The nurse barred their way to the ward. 'You must wait. Dr Kellar already has a visitor. I've just shown her in.'

Faro sprang to his feet. 'Mrs Findlay-Cupar?'

'That is so.'

'Dear God, let's hope we're in time. Come along, McQuinn.'

And, pushing past the startled nurse, Faro ran along the corridor and threw open the door of the ward where Kellar lay.

The woman who stood looking down on the injured

man turned to face them. A woman who looked like a very faded watercolour of Mrs Findlay-Cupar. Faro heard Vince's horrified gasp from behind him.

'Mabel. Mabel! You're alive!'

Chapter Seventeen

Hearing her name, Mabel Kellar ran to Vince, who took her in his arms. Looking across at his stepfather, he made a gesture of helpless bewilderment and led her over to a chair.

Sobbing, she turned to Faro, 'I had to come – I had to come.'

'Mabel Kellar, I am taking you into custody for the attempted murder of your husband, Melville Kellar. Anything you say may be taken down and used in evidence,' said Faro sternly.

She looked at him wide-eyed. 'So you think it was me.'

'We know it was you.'

Suddenly she noticed the travelling bag. She gave a little cry as Faro slipped open the locks. At first glance the bundle he withdrew resembled a tailor's dummy, but closer inspection revealed a padded tunic.

Faro held it up triumphantly. 'Behold the earthly remains of Mrs Flynn.'

Mabel Kellar was suddenly calm. 'All right, I admit it. I wanted him dead. I wanted to punish them both. I could have forgiven him if he hadn't destroyed my baby. Then to give Eveline a child and to want to marry her. I wanted him to suffer as he'd made me suffer through the years. He even told me how easy it would be for him to commit murder and get away with it.

'I decided to beat him at his own game. It seemed so easy. Ever since Christmas I'd been planning my revenge in every detail and Melville played into my hands when he dismissed the last housekeeper. I would pretend to engage a new one, Mrs Flynn. Melville hardly glanced at references and I knew he would never notice the new housekeeper or that he never saw us together. All I had to do was to appear a few times in the kitchen as Mrs Flynn, for Ina's benefit.

'I sent the letter to Tiz. I only intended being Mrs Flynn for a week or so, the longer I kept up the pretext the more dangerous it became, especially as I would have no excuse to remain in the house once Mrs Flynn had worked her notice.'

'All I had to do was disappear, leave some evidence indicating that I had been murdered and then Melville would be convicted and hanged for it.'

'How did you intend to return from the dead?'

'I'd wait a couple of years and pretend to have had a street accident in London and lost my memory. Something like that would work very well,' she said dismissively, while Faro and Vince exchanged helpless glances indicating her extraordinary naivety.

'I had you, Inspector Faro, to the house the night before so that you would be prepared for Mrs Flynn. All I needed were spectacles, a grey wig and a maid's cap. The toothache and swathing my face with scarves was a great help,' she added proudly and then with a sigh, 'No one will ever know how hard it was. I'm not a very good cook at the best of times but it was a nightmare trying to cook for a dinner party and have everything ready at the right time.

'But my plan was working. Next morning Melville took me to the North Berwick train and that was where everything went wrong.'

She stopped and stared miserably out of the window as Faro took up the story.

'When you boarded the train, you were fortunate enough to find an empty first-class compartment. Quickly you took off the fur cloak and became Mrs Flynn, but without the padded tunic because it hampered swift movement. You also had in the bag some raw butcher's meat which you intended to use for dabbing the fur cloak. However, you were unlucky. Another passenger got in. Correct?'

Mrs Kellar nodded dully. 'Yes, at Musselburgh. I decided I must get out at Longniddry and work in the waiting-room, praying that it would be empty. I didn't have a great deal of time if I was to catch the train back to Edinburgh.' She giggled. 'A few minutes, that's all I needed. And then— '

'And then you had your worst bit of luck. You were seen leaving and the man on duty thought you were trying to sneak out without a ticket. When he stopped you, he noticed blood on your hands. While he went for water, you disappeared down the road.'

She shook her head. 'I only went fifty yards, hid round a corner and doubled back and over the railway bridge in time for the Edinburgh train. As we left the station, I waited in the corridor and hurled out the cloak and the knife. If it hadn't been for the snow . . . I began watching the weather. It got worse and worse. And what if someone had decided to keep the cloak? Despite the stains it was valuable – and warm. What if they weren't discovered before Mrs Flynn had worked her notice.'

She paused and laughed bitterly. 'Notice? Melville never noticed me at all, living in the same house. Can you credit that? All he did was leave notes on the table for me. And I hadn't bargained for all that anxiety, those hours of terror when I thought my plan had failed. I couldn't believe that no one would arrest Melville after the cloak and the knife were handed in. It was then I decided on the petticoat.

'If that didn't work, then it would have to be poison. When the postman delivered Eveline's letter, it was like gift from heaven – or hell,' she added savagely. 'My troubles were over. I had been given the perfect reason for his suicide.

'That old pistol, he was very proud of it. I slipped into the bedroom and he was breathing deeply, still asleep, I thought. But as I fired, he opened his eyes, turned his head – oh dear God. He fell back against the pillow. But he wasn't dead.

'He was lying there bleeding to death. And in that moment, I knew how wicked I had been. I knew that I loved him and whatever he had done to me, I wanted him alive again. Especially now that Eveline didn't want him. He would need me again. I would be able to comfort him, prove what a wife's faithful love could be. He would never stray again, he would be so grateful to me for taking him back. And we would be happy,' she added with a wistful sigh and then the tears rolled down her cheeks.

'Oh dear God, what had I done. I had killed him for nothing, nothing,' she added pathetically.

'I must have been out of my mind. I rushed downstairs, got a basin and water – I think I fainted, because when I came to I was lying on the kitchen floor, the water spilt. I refilled it, ran upstairs – and he had gone, bleeding, terribly injured as he was, he had managed to get out of the house.'

She stopped. 'You know the rest.' She looked at Faro. 'I had some other awful moments, when you kept picking up my hair brushes. I was sure you guessed then and I thought Vince had recognised my voice last night.'

'I did – or thought I did,' said Vince.

With a sigh she stood up, 'I'm ready to go with you, but – but I just wanted to see him – just once more.'

She turned to Vince. 'I still love him, even though I wanted my revenge. When I saw him lying dying I knew then that I had only destroyed myself.' Staring across at the bed where Kellar lay, still and inert, she whispered, 'May I kiss him goodbye before I go with you?'

Over her head, Vince nodded eagerly to Faro.

'All right, Mrs Kellar.'

Kellar opened his eyes as she bent over him. 'Mabel – Mabel is that you . . . ?' His voice was faint, far-off. 'I thought you were Flynn.'

She fell sobbing at his bedside. 'Forgive me, forgive me – for loving you.'

Kellar, bewildered, put out a hand and stroked her hair. 'Mabel, you idiot,' he whispered.

Faro and Vince stood by the window watching the motionless couple, the weeping woman whispering at her husband's bedside, holding his hand, his white bandaged face staring straight ahead.

At last, she dried her tears and said, 'I'm ready to go now.'

'Where are you taking her?' asked Kellar weakly. 'Not jail. Oh, no, not until I've talked to Superintendent McIntosh. I've sent for him, he should be here directly.' And in a voice gathering strength, 'Please leave us alone, Faro.'

They joined McQuinn in the corridor and a few minutes later the Superintendent stormed along and, with a face like thunder, motioned Faro towards the waiting-room.

'Mind leaving us, Dr Laurie?' When the door closed, McIntosh sat down and said. 'All right, Faro. Now let's have your version of what all this is about.' He listened grimly and at the end said, 'I'm inclined to agree with your story. But Kellar tells me in confidence that he tried to commit suicide for personal reasons, especially since his wife had gone off and left him.'

It was Faro's turn to look amazed.

'For the record this will go down as an accident with an old pistol he was priming.'

'What about all the evidence, the cloak and the knife, for instance?'

'It will be filed away under mysteries unsolved.'

'And Mrs Flynn?'

'The housekeeper? Oh, she disappeared without leaving a forwarding address. Not unusual where a servant's working notice.'

Faro decided to say nothing of the contents of the travelling bag.

'As for that rather simple maid, we would never call her to give evidence.'

There was a short interval before Faro spoke. 'This is a miscarriage of justice, you understand that, sir, don't you,' he said severely. 'And you are contributing to it.'

McIntosh grinned. 'Of course. But we take our choice and frankly I'd rather distort the truth a little than have the scandal of the Kellar affair, his wife's imprisonment with the inevitable repercussions on the honour of the Edinburgh City Police, made public.'

McIntosh was unlucky. Kellar's accident found its way into the Sunday newspapers and so too did the scandal regarding Mrs Shaw. No one knew quite how or who to blame for 'Sensational story of police surgeon's secret amour. Disappearing wife returns home. After discovering awful truth about her husband's double life . . . '

There was no knighthood possible after that. Mabel could not have had a more perfect revenge since Melville was not only thwarted of honour but also of the woman he had loved and the son he craved, who went with his true father and mother to live in Yorkshire.

Kellar, released from hospital, went home to Mabel.

Vince, although sympathetic, considered it prudent to remain at a distance in future. 'She obviously hadn't even thought it through, had she? I mean, how could she possibly reappear and reclaim all her property without some very searching questions being asked?'

Faro shrugged. 'I don't think it would have ever got that far. The moment she knew Kellar had been convicted, she would never have let him hang. Not after that performance when he was only injured.'

'What would she have got, if he'd let her be taken? Not the death sentence, I hope,' said Vince.

'A few years for attempted murder.'

Vince sighed. 'Poor Mabel. Her sentence has already begun.'

'Yes, lad, it began by his bedside and I'm afraid it will continue for the rest of her life.'